NOTHING BUT BLOOD

NOTHING BUT BLOOD

PAULINE C. SMITH

CUTTING EDGE

ISBN-13: 978-1-957868-20-2

Published by
Cutting Edge Books
PO Box 8212
Calabasas, CA 91372
www.cuttingedgebooks.com

CHAPTER ONE

The room was a sullen guard, defending the secrets of its transient owners with soiled impersonality. It spoke only through the almost obliterated pattern of its carpet, through smudged marks about its light switch where countless fingers had fumbled on countless nights.

The overhead bulb, shaded by frosted glass, formed a shining cemetery for the little death piles of insects. The small bier above cast a shadow on the eyes of a man beneath it. His face looked like a blank sheet of paper until he moved his weight so that his eyes, in the light, became a police depatment's letterhead on the unwritten page.

"Not pretty," he announced as he turned away.

The other, perfect contrast to his companion; his body trivial by comparison, rigid in its intensity; his face a scrawled and rewritten epic, showed the snarl of sorrow in his mind.

"Not pretty," he agreed.

Nor was she, the girl in the valley of the bed, snuggled into its contours in a cozy kind of chill. Her tongue protruded at the forces of the law. Her eyes glinted in reflection of the death pyre above.

The smaller man shuddered. "Never can get used to it," he said almost to himself. "It's always new and always grim."

"Death?" The big man turned to inspect the dresser.

"Violent death. Find anything, Barclay?"

"Not yet."

The frayed towel on the dresser top was like a sheet of snow empty of tracks to show where the traveler was headed or why she had stopped her journey.

"No perfume. No powder. No nothing."

Barclay yanked open a drawer, lifting the pink things to shake them vigorously. "Not many panties." He pushed the drawer closed and tried another. "Laine—"

Together, they leaned over the bag of cracked, simulated leather. On the unruffled white towel of the dresser top, they laid its contents—a battered lipstick case with only a small wedge of crimson paste left; a compact, the cake powder worn to silver in the center; a stub of pencil and a blue handkerchief smudged in the corner as if it had been wound around a tidy finger and used to dust the toe of a shoe. That was all.

Barclay laid the handbag on the dresser.

"No money? No money at all?" asked Laine, his thin fingers crawling through the fabrics in the drawer.

"Probably whoever did that," Barclay gestured toward the bed, "took it, if there was any."

"Here's a billfold." From the crumpled material, Laine lifted it, a coin purse with wallet attached. He opened it up and beside the bits of possession on the dresser, counted out the money. "Ten. Eleven. And the change. Eleven dollars and thirty-five cents. Did the fingerprint boys put everything back the way they found it?"

"Yep. Said so. Guess the billfold wasn't in the pocketbook. Probably the killer was in a hurry, threw things around. Guess he didn't want cash. Just wanted to finish her off and get rid of identification."

"Looks that way." Laine was gazing at the cellophane pocket which bulged as if it had once held not only identification, but other papers as well. He dropped the bit of leather to the dresser and dusted his fingers.

Barclay was again shaking garments. From a sleazy slip, its parted threads too tired to longer hold a secret, slithered a bright flash of color to snake down Barclay's trouser leg and nestle into its cuff.

Both men stooped.

"There," pointed Laine.

Barclay inserted his thumb and forefinger and from the cuff of his trouser, held up a short length of beads, little blue teardrops on a string. He wound it around his wrist. The ribbon ends, extending from the beads on either side, met with only a little left over.

"Not a necklace," said Barclay, "too short."

"Bracelet?" offered Laine.

Barclay shook his head. "It looks familiar. I've seen the same things somewhere."

He dangled the bauble under the shadowed glow of light. As the beads twisted, coy letters peeped out from the colored squares. Barclay turned to Laine. "That's it," he said. His face was still blank and the upturned corners of his lips a parenthesis around nothing. He jiggled the little boxes of glass. "Baby's beads."

Laine frowned, looking at the short blue strand dangling from pudgy fingers.

"New born baby's beads," continued Barclay. "They put 'em on 'em in the hospital."

"What for?"

"Identification."

Barclay pushed aside the lipstick and compact on the dresser to lay the beads flat on the white towel. He turned them until the white letters shone from the blue squares. They spelled BARNES. "See!" said Barclay, "Barnes. That's the pappy's name of the baby who belongs to this—presumably."

"Are you sure?"

Barclay grinned, but it did not alter his expression. "Well, I'm not sure that this name means it's the baby's pappy—it's a wise father, you know. But I am sure that this string of beads hung on some newborn baby. Hell, I've seen 'em three times on my own kids. I ought to know."

"Wonder if they were the girl's, or if she had a child?"

Barclay shrugged. "Who knows? We can get the doctor to tell us if she's ever been a mother. That might help."

"Too bad Barnes is such a common name."

"Yeah. Why couldn't it have been Zwifflehoffer or Gritzenvanheim?"

"Not enough beads. Wonder what they do when there are too many letters?"

Barclay shrugged again. He crumpled the beads into a heap and walked to the closet. "Not much here, either. Coat, hat, a pair of shoes and a suit."

Together, they draped the few garments over the end railing of the bed, carefully respectful not to touch the twisted nylon tones of the corpse. A small hole in the ankle of fabric had started to ladder up cold flesh.

"No labels," said Barclay. "The killer probably got rid of them."

Laine held the coat high. "This is cheap stuff. Never were any labels." He shook the garment and pried his fingers into its pockets. Gently, he waved a crumpled handkerchief, and from its crushed folds a small wisp of newspaper fluttered to the floor. Laine laid the coat on the bed to pick up the torn fragment and smoothed it in the palm of his hand. "This is a death notice," he said, "and there's a telephone number penciled in the margin."

Barclay looked over his shoulder.

The item was terse. "Nurse Carlotta Conti, of the Parkway Maternity Hospital, suffered a fatal heart attack while on duty today. Funeral arrangements pending."

Laine turned the paper to its other side to stare a moment at a few ruptured words of department store ad. He flipped it back. "Must be the nurse she was interested in. Or the telephone number. Or both." He looked up into the blank face of his companion. "Where's the Parkway? You know?"

Barclay shrugged.

"Well, how about the H.A. number. Is there an exchange around like that?"

"Could be the Valley. There's a HAnover number there. Maybe that's where the Parkway is."

Laine snapped the fragment of paper with an impatient fingernail. "It's where a lot of big aircraft companies are, too. Maybe she was just looking for a job. It'd be our luck this item's nothing but a hunk of paper she tore out to write down a fluke telephone number."

Again Barclay shrugged. Laine pouted his lips. The corners of his eyelids crinkled. "The Parkway might be around here. Might be somewhere else."

"Yeah."

A weak, experimental knock sounded at the door, the knuckles tentative, wishing they were somewhere else. The two men turned, their faces covered over the masks of authority.

"Yeah?" grunted Barclay.

Opening a wedge, the door widened to let wizened features peer through. The fringe of hair above the corrugation of forehead was upraised as if it, too, were frightened. "I'm the manager." The words jumped through the mouth in little scared leaps. "The doctor just come—" His eyes darted one forbidden glance at the bed. "—for her." Then he hugged his teeth with his lips as if afraid they'd get chilled.

"Okay. Send him in," said Barclay.

Laine stepped forward. "Go back down to your desk and stay there. I want to talk with you." The manager ducked and fled, to let the doctor with his stretcher bearers through.

The doctor was tall and spare. He bent over the bed like paper folding in the middle. His eyes took in the bruises of the corpse's neck, just beginning to show their dirty marks. He grunted.

"With a pillowslip. They either do it with a pillowslip or a silk stocking. Always the same." He looked at the pillow where the girl's long blonde hair sprayed on the smudged ticking, and distended his nostrils toward the room. "Always in some hole, too. Everybody through with her now?" he asked the officers.

Barclay nodded. "She's all yours."

"When you post her," added Laine, "check and see if she's ever had a baby."

The doctor showed a skeletal smile. "Why? You lose track of one of yours?"

Laine looked sulky. "Don't be funny."

"Okay, boys," said the doctor. "roll her on."

The stretcher bearers went to work. Laine watched the arms flip and the body sag as it was lifted to the stretcher. The girl's limp head rolled toward him, the tongue bunching out.

As the doctor followed the burden through the door, he turned. "I'll check that, Laine. You boys can drop around tomorrow afternoon. I'll have the dope for you then."

The door snapped shut.

CHAPTER TWO

Laine leaned against the grimy desk in the dim hotel lobby. The cluster lights overhead and the electric candle fixtures on the wall scattered shadows to the corners. The manager's fingers trembled over the register, large knuckles dancing to a tempo of their own.

He twisted the book around. "Here it is," he said, pointing. "This is her signature."

Laine pushed the finger aside to look down at the childish scrawl. "Mary Barnes." BARNES, just as the square blue beads had proclaimed. "She gives her address as Los Angeles." He looked up at the manager.

"That's all I know, Mister. Just what they write down. Maybe she was from here. Maybe she wasn't." He tried a smile to see if it would work.

"No luggage? Other than the small bag upstairs?"

"No. Nothing else."

Laine's finger moved along the registry date. "Hmm. Been here four days. Know if she spent much time in her room?"

"I don't think so, sir. I think she was generally gone all day. She just come back to sleep."

"Did you find her?"

The manager looked wild-eyed as if the investigator had asked him to go back in time and discover the dead, cold thing. "No. My night clerk. He found her."

"Where is he?"

"He's in bed. Made him sick, I guess. Vomited all over the hall after he saw her." The manager's face turned a faint chartreuse and Laine stepped back from the desk, eyes wary. "He made a report to the first men, the policemen, when they come."

"Okay. Tell me about it."

"Well, the night clerk got a complaint from the woman that has the next room. The next room, I mean, to that girl's ..."

Laine nodded.

"There was a radio goin'. Loud. And it was eleven-thirty—"

Laine moved close to the desk again. "Radio? I saw no radio in that room."

"No, sir. There wasn't none. The girl didn't have one." He widened his eyes righteously. "We don't have radios in the rooms. Noisy."

Laine looked around at the moth-eaten fixtures of the lobby. Solemnly, he nodded.

"I don't know where the radio come from, or even if there was one. I only know about the complaint. The desk clerk said he'd do something about it. Then he got busy. He didn't get up there for fifteen or twenty minutes—"

"What'd he get busy at? At eleven-thirty at night?"

"Well—a drunk come in—that happens—"

"Okay. Then what?"

The manager spread his shaking hands. "Well, then, he just found her like you saw her. He used a passkey to get in, and she was just a-layin' there. Her tongue—well, she was just a-layin' there."

"The room was locked then, and no one else in there?"

"That's it. Her key's gone, too. So I guess whoever did it took it with him."

"How about visitors? Surely the desk clerk saw someone come down, or knew who went up. Don't visitors have to inquire here before they go up?"

This was what had worried the manager. This was the creeping question which had finally raised its head to dart forth a forked tongue. "Well, you know how it is," he offered lamely.

"No. How is it?"

"At night everything's quiet. People come and go. I guess the desk clerk just didn't pay any attention." "Is that a habit of this crummy hotel—to let people go up and down at will?" Laine's voice had grown hard. "Don't you insist that your tenants leave their keys when they go out and call for them when they return?"

"I do," said the manager. "But employees are careless. That, I can't help."

"Self-service elevator," observed Laine, his eyes wandering to the gilt-pocked cage, "and a stairway." He lifted his hat from the desk. "Well, when your night clerk gets over his tizzy, I'll have a little talk with him." He put on the hat, adjusted it. "The door to the girl's room is locked Stay out of it."

The manager nodded.

"The Police Department told you. Now the Sheriff's Office is telling you."

"How long," faltered the manager," will it have to be that way? I lose money on a room that ain't occupied. People come in all the time and want—" His words broke off before Laine's fanged grin.

"As long as we need it."

The manager gulped, tried again. "This hotel's got a good name," he began.

"I'll bet."

"I'm just wonderin' what will be in the papers."

"Don't worry. This is a big, mean city. People get killed in it all the time. The item'll probably be about an inch long… 'Girl, registered as Mary Barnes, found dead in downtown hotel. The Sheriffs Office is assisting the City Police in an investigation to determine if the death is suicide or murder'."

"Suicide? Cripes. She couldn'ta done that to herself."

Laine leaned over and patted a location of air above the manager's shoulder. "Bright boy. You know it and I know it. Now keep your mouth shut and that door locked." He walked across the rug of the hotel lobby, little clouds of dust following each heel print.

Out on the pavement, dirty dawn was just breaking through the black curtain of night. Small gusts of wind raised bits of paper in the gutters. Trucks had started to move on the next street, which was the margin between the old residential section of Los Angeles and the new industrial province.

Laine yawned and stepped into his coupe. The hours had limped by as slowly as if they had lead in their minutes.

He rolled down streets pallid as a tired prostitute, streets which had a hard night and were finding it difficult to come awake. Again through his mind passed the thought. This was a tough job: this ferreting out of the killers of the killed. He wished he were a mailman or a grocery clerk.

CHAPTER THREE

"She's in the morgue now, boys, if you want to see her again."

"Why would we want to see her again?" asked Barclay.

The doctor inhaled deeply and the smoke fell heavily from his nostrils. Laine could almost see its circular journey through translucent skin. "She looks better. I stuck her tongue back in her mouth and closed her eyes. Fine looking girl. You'd be surprised."

"I'm not surprised at anything," said Laine.

"Young, too. Can't be over twenty-one -two. Just a kid."

"Strangulation?" asked Barclay.

"That's right. There was an X slashed on her breast, but it was just there for decoration -not serious. Laine, she'd been a mother, all right."

"Yes?"

"She'd had a hard time, too. She'll never have another baby."

"Of course she won't. She's dead."

"I mean, if she'd lived, she couldn't have had another. She'd had a hard enough time having the one she had. I'd say she delivered about two—three years ago. Difficult to tell, though. I'm going by scar tissue and the look of the stitches."

"Well, that's that." Laine stood up.

"Sure you don't want to go down and look at her?" The doctor glanced up brightly, his fibrous neck jutting eagerly from its collar.

Barclay laughed. "No. We got work to do. Why don't you go?"

"No, boys." The doctor lost interest and turned back to his desk. "Got to be going. Knife-wound down at the jail. The kid'll need a dressing."

Barclay followed Laine into the corridor.

"Damn ghoul," said Laine. "I wouldn't put it past him to knock over somebody just so he could be in at the death."

"You're sensitive," said Barclay. "He's a good doctor. He just likes his work."

"Maybe he should be a mortician."

Barclay chuckled. "I'll suggest it to him. Trouble is, he might get slipped into the box by mistake. It would be an easy goof to make."

"That's no lie. You call that Hanover number?"

"Yeah. Know what I got?"

"Lockheed"

"No. I got a school board."

Laine whirled, staring at Barclay. "A school board, for God's sake?"

Barclay nodded. "Central office. There was a telephone operator there. She didn't know from nothin'. She told me the number is one of the High Schools, but there won't be anybody there until after the Christmas Holidays—"

"Fine," said Laine without expression.

"I asked her if the name Conti rang a bell—thought maybe she might have been a school nurse. It didn't."

"Probably hasn't anything to do with the case at all," said Laine. "Like I said, maybe the Barnes girl just tore out that particular scrap of paper to have something to write the telephone number on."

"So," said Barclay, "I asked her if she'd ever heard of a girl called Mary Barnes."

"And she hadn't." predicted Laine.

"No. She hadn't."

Laine walked a few steps down the corridor. "Did you contact the nurses' registry?"

"Yeah. The woman there said she'd look up the dope."

"Let's go."

They rolled down city streets bright with sun and busy with shoppers. "We'll park here," said Laine, "and walk. My God! What a crowd!"

Barclay lumbered from the car to follow.

"Christmas," he mumbled, "I gotta get some shoppin' done too."

The building was cool inside and remotely quiet. They pushed open a heavy, well-oiled door to step onto a thick turf of carpet.

A horse-faced woman with buck-teeth as white as her starched cap waited for them behind the desk. She smiled a welcome as warm as a burnt-out electric blanket.

"I called about Carlotta Conti," began Barclay.

Briskly, the woman nodded, her finger traveling down lines of inked writing on the sheets spread before her. She looked up with a penetrating glance through her bifocals. "Miss Conti was on our registry pages from 1941 to February of '51—"

Barclay turned his expressionless face toward Laine. "So maybe she *is* a part of this deal."

He asked the woman, "And after '51?" She shrugged her shoulders, her short upper lip rising over the white porcelain squares in her mouth.

"You mean you have no further record on her?" Laine stepped forward to lean over the desk."Well, does that mean she moved away? Just stopped being a nurse? Or did she slip some arsenic to old lace?"

She didn't think it was funny. She pursed her lips. "It could," she said, embracing one or all of Laine's suggestions. "Or, maybe," she added, "there was a scandal. Then, of course, we wouldn't allow her to register."

"You just cross 'em off then," said Barclay, teetering his bulk. "No explanation on your records?"

"None here." The woman clacked her teeth as if she were through with the matter. "We never placed her again after '51. That's all I know."

Laine pushed close. "Is there anyone around this Florence Nightingale warehouse who'd know why the Conti character got the bounce?"

"No."

"What happens then? Suppose she gave someone a goof ball instead of an aspirin, and they lopped her head off? What then? Suppose she's got a one-track mind and can't do anything except read thermometers?"

"In that case," said the woman, speaking toward a corner of the room," although we couldn't place her, nor would any other accredited agency, she might work on her own, seeking out private cases -or under cover in a questionable institution."

Laine turned toward Barclay. "The Parkway," he said. He leaned over the desk. "Ever hear of it? Parkway Maternity Hospital?"

The woman turned the thought over. Then she reached out for a heavy book. Leafing the pages rapidly, she peered through her glasses at the lines of print. Looking up, she shook her head. "Not listed."

Laine's shoulders sagged.

"It might be a rest home. Or a nursing home operating without license." She closed the book with a brisk snap. "There are a lot of them. Every place."

"That's it." Laine stepped back. "They're every place. And the newspaper clipping might be from any newspaper. Come on, Barclay."

Out in the corridor, Laine snorted. "That woman in there remembered more about Conti than she was giving out."

Barclay shrugged.

"I ought to go back in there and make her tell what she knows. She acted like she was thinking about naughty words out behind the barn." Laine half turned.

"Skip it," said Barclay. "Conti may not mean anything after all. Like you said, It may be just a piece of paper."

CHAPTER FOUR

Greasy, eye-smarting, throat-stinging smog hung in the sunshine and sneaked through the windows. Barclay mopped his brow and blew his nose. "Hot for December and the smog's gettin' worse."

"It'll start raining any time now and wash the air," said Laine. "Well, that much is that." He stretched, pushing the heavy newspaper file back on the table. "So Conti took the rap."

Barclay widened his eyes. "You don't think she did the operation on the Claridge girl?"

"I think the doctor did. Conti was the nurse, that's all. She took the rap to protect him. Maybe for love. Maybe for some other price." Laine rapped the newspaper gently. "This Ten Eyck was a society doctor. Rich. Well, they get rich on neurotics. They get rich on little nymphos like the Claridge dish, too." He leaned over, watching Barclay closely. "You know what this Claridge girl was?"

"Sure. She was a lush. A pretty little spoiled lush all wrapped up in mink."

"That's right. And all wrapped up in her parents' dough, too. You know these scrapes she got into and all the money-lined hush-hush the authorities waded through … well, she was a nympho, too. Poor nymphs get all messed up by some quack, or have their babies and leave them. Rich nymphos get rid of theirs at the hands of a doctor like Ten Eyck—behind closed doors—see nothing, hear nothing, tell nothing—unless something goes wrong, of course—" He tapped the newspaper. "Like it did in this case.

Then the whole thing blows wide open and maybe some nurse steps in and takes the blame—"

"What's a nympho?"

Laine grinned. "Why Junior, I should drop dead for letting you in on some of the more beautifully sordid facts of life, but a nympho is a little skirt that can't hang onto it—a bad little girl, Junior." He brooded a moment with a hurt look. "I've never been lucky enough to meet one socially. But it's my ambition."

Barclay's face showed neither understanding or puzzlement.

"Now maybe Conti did perform this operation on the Claridge girl." conceded Laine. "But I'll bet my front teeth the doctor did. The girl was rich—so why get some nurse to do the work? Doctors can be bribed—or maybe Ten Eyck had a reputation for it already. I say, since he dropped his practice in that millionaire's paradise like a hot potato, he was beating the gun. Either things had broken or he figured they would any minute."

"Well, maybe," Barclay wasn't sure.

Laine stood. "He's still in the county, if this directory is right. That province is mine. I'll check up on him while you connect the high school."

Barclay looked up, startled. "Who do I see at the high school?"

Laine grinned down at him. "Who do you usually see in a high school? Didn't you go to high school?"

"Sure." Barclay scowled combatively. "I spent most of my time in the principal's office."

Laine laughed. "That's where you go now. You go to the principal's office and ask the principal why Mary Barnes was carrying around the school's telephone number." Tenderly, he tapped his teeth with a fingernail. "There's got to be a reason for the telephone number."

"But this is Christmas vacation."

"I guess you'll have to go to the school board and find out who's principal. I guess you'll have to do some leg work."

"Hell," said Barclay.

A policeman walked through the door, his face a cheerful cherub's. "I found that item you wanted, sir," he said to Barclay.

"The Conti death notice?"

"Yes, sir. The paper's two weeks old."

"Let's see it." Barclay extended his hand and took the long binding edge which held the newspapers together. Laine stepped close to look over his shoulder.

"Looks like it," said Laine. "Turn it over and see if that ad's on the other side."

"Yep. I guess this is it."

"Well," said Laine, "the Parkway isn't far away, then. I think that's Ten Eyck's set-up and I've got a hunch it's close to where he lives—somewhere around that address out there in the county that's listed in the directory. Want to bet?"

Barclay shook his head.

CHAPTER FIVE

The sky was a low gray ceiling, suspended by ominous black beams as Laine drove through the Valley and toward the pass. As he rose, on the ribbon of road, the beams flattened out and drops began to fall. Foggy mist swirled about the car, and Laine leaned over to snap the windshield wiper into action. It switched back and forth, an angry tail of vision. He hugged the bank as he ascended, away from the drop with its rising vapor.

At the top, where the ground stretched wide on each side. Laine stopped the car at a turn-off to light a cigarette. The rain slashed down in wide armfuls and wet fingers of it crawled through the window. Laine rolled the glass closed and shivered.

"Roast yesterday and freeze today," he commented aloud. He turned on the dash light. With the cigarette in the corner of his mouth sending up thin spirals of smoke, he consulted his map. It was four o'clock and almost dark.

By six, he had sloshed into several wrong turns and circled a detour.

At six-fifteen, his headlights caught ghostly fence palings through their indecisive beams. "Goddamned weather," he complained as he turned the car cautiously from asphalt to gravel.

Under the carport, he opened the door. Water rained down upon his knees as he twisted from the driver's seat. "Goddamned business to be in."

He flicked the beam of his flash to light up the small metal plate on the door ... "MAURICE X. TEN EYCK, M.D."

While he could still hear the faint chimes in the house after pressing the button, his flash darted prying rays of light about him. "Big and beautiful," he labelled the house.

As the door opened a stingy space, Laine set his foot heavily in the crack.

"Dr. Ten Eyck."

The hawklike face peering out at him from the gold warmth of the room into the cold light of his flash, sharpened. "Not in," said the maid.

"Mrs. Ten Eyck, then." Laine was being patient about it. He leaned his small wiry strength nonchalantly against the heavy panels of the door, and worked his foot farther through the widening gap.

"Mrs. Ten Eyck—"

"I know," anticipated Laine, "Mrs. Ten Eyck doesn't see anybody." With a quick twist, he was inside. He backed up against the door and heard it click behind him. "Except tonight she'll see somebody. She'll see me."

The maid faded down the hall and to the rear.

While he waited in the corridor of warmth, Laine felt the comfort of the house pat him gently on the chill damp of his shoulders. As soon as the woman entered, she turned him cold again. She carried her ravaged madonna face carefully, the draperies of her gown floating about her like a cloud.

Laine looked her over with the feeling that he saw only the dried pod of a woman, forgotten and left on the tree to wither. Then, at the dying ember of fire in her eye, he wondered if there might not be a time bomb inside her just waiting for the moment when an explosion would be magnificent.

"Dr. Ten Eyck," he said, "I wanted to see him." He spoke his words carefully, rounding the vowels and clicking the consonants, hoping to get through the layers and years of seclusion. "I came clear out from Los Angeles to contact him."

No response.

"I thought if I couldn't get him here at his home, maybe I could see him at the hospital. The Parkway Hospital."

The woman did not stir.

Laine clenched his fists. "I know the hospital's a private one, but I thought maybe the name of Carlotta Conti could get me in."

Only the eyelids fluttered in the life-scarred face.

"So she's dead. Had a heart attack. So my timing's wrong. She told me about the doctor—how did I know she was going to die and leave me without an entrance ticket?"

As Laine watched the woman's face closely, he saw it open a moment, like the petals of a withered flower.

"Look, Mrs. Ten Eyck—" He reached over to grasp her arm with his thumb and forefinger. "Tell me how to get to the doctor. Believe me, it's important."

Like a sleepwalker, rousing, but not yet fully awake she looked down first at his urgent hand and then into his tense face.

"I've got to see him. Do you understand that? You're a doctor's wife. Have you forgotten—?" He gave a slight tug to her arm, and the words and gentle jerk acted like snapped fingers before her face.

First, she looked startled. Then her temple lay flat and smooth. The ruins of her face became quiet. "Take this road until it turns off, about a quarter of a mile on down the hill. Follow it until you come to the first lane. That's to your right. You'll come to a small grove of trees. You'll have to park your car there and walk through. That's where the hospital is."

Laine turned and opened the door. He looked back, wishing he could help this woman to live and feel and laugh again, but he knew it was too late. He'd entered a nine o'clock movie at ten-thirty, he thought, and the picture was almost over.

He stepped through the door and turned once more to look back into the gold-washed interior of the house. The entrance hall was empty. He felt his spine quiver as he walked into the gusty night and closed the door behind him. With the rising wind, the coupe swayed down the dark road. He drove past the lane before he saw it. He backed to peer through the darkness. The car wheels spun as they struck slick adobe.

The grove of trees appeared so quickly, his brakes squealed through the low roar of wind. He braced himself, stepping to the ground.

The wind whipped his topcoat about him like a rumpled skin. His feet slid along clay until he came to the shelter of trees which formed an island of silence, cutting off the growl of the wind and forming a carpet of leaves for his steps.

Before him crouched a shadow deeper than those of the night, with oblong chinks of light shining through like slitted eyes watching his approach. "This is a real good night for a mad surgeon," thought Laine. "Maybe I'll end up with my brains in a bottle." He tapped his coat pocket. The hard lump there gave him a sense of reassurance if not contentment.

The wide porch with its entrance doors separated itself from the gloom as he came closer. Laine had his hands dug deep in his side pockets, one resting about the handle of a gun, the other with a fingertip on the snap of the flash light. His steps lagged up the three terrace stairs, then like the sudden jolt of surprise, hard light flashed. He looked up. The porch was ablaze with electricity. Pressing his lips tight, the satyr took over the whole of his face.

Just as he reached it, the door opened. Laine's fingers tightened around the handle of the gun. "Expecting me?" he asked harshly. Then his expression gentled.

The man before him was hardly a man. He looked as if he had finished with all that and was just waiting to step into the neuter-state beyond.

Laine pushed inside and backed against the door, his hands still deep in his pockets. His eyes flicked the corners of the reception room. He gave a soundless whistle. This place had none of the lulling come-on of an ordinary hospital. This was cold business. Three straight-backed chairs stood in a no-nonsense line. The desk was flanked by shelves for account books.

His eyes came back to the shrinking nonentity before him. "Well, you're not Ten Eyck," he said with certainty.

The rumpled coveralls, the large-pupiled eyes, the dirty fingers, all jumped to energetic attention. "You got a woman out there in your car? You want I should bring in some bags? You want I should call the doctor so you can pay for things?"

At that moment, an inner door opened and through it walked a man so handsome Laine did not believe him. All the results of his looks were pressed on his face with a cool iron -vanity -egotism and self indulgence, centered with a widow's peak that gave him an unnatural symmetry so that Laine remembered a speech he had once heard about dividing and judging faces... "And always," the speaker had said with conviction, "you'll find the bad side and the good side." Not so, thought Laine, not in this case.

"Don't leave, Pop. There may be work for you." Then the man condescended to speak to Laine. "I'm Dr. Ten Eyck. Did you want to see me?"

"Well, yes," said Laine. "I did." He had the feeling he was not talking to a man, but to a conventional design with manicured nails and an immaculate white linen jacket. "You're a hard man to see what with your unlisted hospital and your house 'way out at the end of hell-and-gone. You're such a hard man to see that I figure maybe you don't want people to see you."

The doctor's eyebrow climbed, upsetting the symmetry of his face.

Laine rocked on the balls of his feet, his hand still in his pocket nursing the gun. "I wouldn't want to see you except for nurse Carlotta Conti, who is dead now -and I wouldn't be interested in *her* except for Mary Barnes. I *am* interested in Mary Barnes," and Laine stressed the point. "Therefore, I'm interested in Carlotta Conti because Mary Barnes was interested enough in her to carry a news clipping around with her. Which comes again to you. Now that Conti's dead, I'm interested in you."

Laine couldn't tell from Ten Eyck's face whether he was thinking of an answer to give or whether he was going to let the whole thing go and not answer at all.

"To refresh your memory, Mary Barnes had a baby removed in this—" he looked around the austere reception room," hospital just about three years ago."

The long shot hit home in the doctor's eyes. "That's quite a history you gave me," he said suavely. "I don't understand any of it and I never heard of a Mary Barnes in my life."

"Okay then you won't mind my having a look at your book of incoming patients for 1951."

Ten Eyck's mouth curved around a blank. "You haven't any authority to walk in here and ask to see my books."

Inside the pocket, Laine's forefinger tapped against the metal of the gun. "I've got authority."

Ten Eyck's eyes dropped and raised again. "Of course, if you try strong arm tactics..." Fluidly, he moved around the desk. Laine stood across from him, the polished wood a barrier between them. The doctor reached down.

Plucking the gun from his pocket, Laine laid it on the desk, his thumb nervously polishing the handle, his forefinger resting on the trigger. A quick glance toward his right, convinced him the wraith was only an interested bystander, his eyes beady with curiosity.

"I want to look at the 1951 book," repeated Laine, "along about the time you started this health and happiness joint—then, after I find out about that, we'll go on a little inspection tour—"

Ten Eyck, stooping, showed only his eyes along the top edge of the bookcase. They contracted, the wrinkled corners looking like a jigsaw puzzle he had almost solved. He hoisted a book between them. It looked like a hotel registry. The date on the outside titled it May, 1951 to May, 1952.

Laine nodded. "That would probably be your fiscal year. It'd take you about three months to get out of your hot water in L. A. and establish this set-up out here." Laine pushed an obstruction out of his way. A small portable radio.

Whirling the book around so the investigator could could open it, the doctor said, "This is just a hobby of mine. All of this. It's my laboratory. I do research work now."

"Yeah?" said Laine. He held the gun in his right hand, turning the pages with his left.

"This search of yours," said Ten Eyck, "won't do you any good.

Laine's eyes ran down the Joneses and the Smiths. His lip curled.

"I don't know what your motive is," said the doctor, "but if you think you're going to pin anything on me—"

"MARY BARNES" Laine's. forefinger traveled to the date of her admittance, July 3, 1951. His head was lowered, his eyes staring at this link in the chain, when out of the storm of the night, the ceiling toppled on his skull. Thunder roared. Lightning sparkled. Reluctantly, he felt himself sag against the desk. He heard the tear of paper. He closed his fist and let go. Through a pinpoint of light in the blank curtain of his mind, threadlike tones penetrated the trowl of his unconsciousness.

"But how'll I get back?" The thin voice squealed like chalk on the blackboard of his conception.

"You'll walk, dammit. Here's some brandy. Keep you warm. Come on, Pop. I'll give you some pretty dreams when you get back.

Laine felt himself lifted. Then he felt no more.

CHAPTER SIX

Events galloped through Laine's subconscious...a head hunter grabbed him by a tuft of hair...a flame eater poked a lighted torch down his throat....Laine leaped, roaring, and pulled himself into wakeful nightmare.

Wildly, he looked at the glowing dome light of his car, and then at the face bent over him in grotesque shadow. "By God," he growled weakly, "you're the joker let me into that fun house."

"There now, it was the brandy brought you 'round," said Pop. "Good old brandy," and took a swig himself, wiped the back of his hand across cracked lips, capped the bottle and slipped it into his pocket. "Bottled muscles. Bottled guts. Bottled—Well, anyway, it got you here, right in you li'l ol car where Pop and the brandy brought you. Feel better?"

Laine noticed then that it wasn't the storm outside that pelted his head, but the sound of it beating against the pain. Carefully, he searched his skull with delicate fingers.

"Won't be no bump," said his companion. "The doc's smart. He knows where to conk so it won't leave a mark." He chuckled. "He'll see there ain't no mark in your memory, either. At least, not so anybody else can notice it. You a cop?"

Laine looked at the face too close to his own. Like a dirty, dried lemon, he thought. There wasn't enough padding under the flesh to hide the errors of the skeleton. Laine felt in his pocket. The gun was gone. He edged back, his fingers slipping around his flashlight. "I'm an investigator from the Sheriff's Office."

The face grinned, showing its sepia teeth. "Same thing. You're still a cop, Know how I know?" The face pushed closer. Laine lifted his nostrils tidily, folding them back against the nearness.

"How?"

"'Cause I was one once. Yep." He drew out the bottle again, waved it toward Laine. Laine shook his head. Pop tasted it, rolled the drops around on his tongue and once more slipped it in hiding. "Got in a little trouble, though. They put me away." The bony saffron fingers reached into the gloomy air to pick a piece of nothing from it.

Laine's eyes grew knowing. "Narcotics," he supplied.

"Yep. That's right." Pop grew thoughtful. "The stuff'll shove me right in the box some day. But it's worth it." He turned crafty. "The girl you were asking about. The Barnes girl..."

Laine drew a mask over his face and waited.

"I can tell you about her."

"She looked like a daughter I once had." He jerked his head quickly and peered at Laine. "You tryin' to help her?"

"The Barnes girl? Yes."

"Okay, then. Listen. I ain't got much time." He looked over his shoulder in the sanctuary of the car. "This girl come to the hospital about three years ago." Laine rolled a piece of paper, balled and wet, around in the palm of his hand. "Some stiff-necked squirt that looked like a professor brought her and left her like she was an extra head he was ashamed of or something. She was nuts about him, you could tell, and she shouldn'ta wasted her time with such a cold fish. You could tell that, too." Pop's fingers made an aimless pattern. "Well, she had her kid. Little girl, I think. She was crazy 'bout it, too... but, of course, she couldn't keep it. It was one of those things. So they adopted it out."

"That's the racket there, isn't it?" Laine's voice was soft to keep the threads of the woven spell intact.

"Yep. Black market babies. Lot of dough in it. Doc got a nice piece of change out o' that little deal."

"Who did the child go to?"

"Don't know. Someone important. Lots of excitement when that doctor from L. A. come steamin' in for the baby."

"What doctor?"

"Oh, I dunno. Some high monkey-monk." Pop chuckled. "That was his name. Monkey Monk."

"Go on."

"Well, after they took the baby, they shoved the Barnes girl out with a few bucks. She went all right, but I dunno, maybe she got thinkin' about that kid o' hers. I can see how it'd be. I get to thinkin' about mine. My girl died when she was about the age of Mary Barnes ... that's what started me off—"

"Back to the Barnes girl."

Pop reached up to grab a piece of seeping fog. "Anyway, she wanted the kid back. You know they don't have no adoption papers or nothin'. Well, she come back here 'bout two weeks ago and raised an awful stink with the doc. He threw her out. But I seen her later in the grove talkin' to the Conti woman."

Laine snapped his fingers.

"That Conti dame, you know was sure nuts about the doc."

"That's about the way I figured it," said Laine softly.

"I heard 'em talkin'. Seems she took some rap for him once. So she pretty much run the joint here and he had to keep his trap shut. This time, though, he shut hers but good. I was listenin' outside the door. It was right after Conti had got through talkin' to the Barnes girl, and she left. Conti told the doc she'd squealed to her."

Laine leaned forward. "You mean she told Mary Barnes where her baby was?"

"I guess so. Doc got fightin' mad. He whaled away at her and knocked her down. Bowie! That was the last of Conti."

"You mean he killed her?"

Pop stiffened, virtuously. "Doc wouldn't kill." Then he pulled a figment of imagination from his coat lapel. "Too rough ... and ticklish. He just pasted her one. Bad heart. All he had to do then was sit there and not give her anything. Her bad heart did the rest."

"You knew this? And you didn't help the nurse?"

Pop shrugged. "That's the doc's department. I don't see nothin' or hear nothin'. Then I get my stuff to keep my *own* heart goin'. Savvy?"

"Yes. Yes. I think I do. Here. I'll drive you back to that lane. Then I'm headed for L. A."

"Oh, no you don't." Pop opened the car door and the sound of rain rushed in. He backed out into the downpour. "I was supposed to leave you on the highway and walk back. That's what I'm doin'. Doc'll know just by how wet my clothes are if I've done what he said to do."

"Okay, then. Suffer." Laine kicked the motor alive.

Pop was closing the door. When there was enough of it left open for his head to shine through, he said, "If you come back to investigate, the doc'll have quite a story about that conk on your head. You won't be able to find any loopholes. He'll prob'ly let you through the hospital, too. And there prob'ly won't be any patients and there won't be any babies. Just watch. You'll see."

The door snapped shut. Laine turned his car around. The thump on his head had changed from staccato tack beats to velvet hammer strokes.

"Yes," he said thoughtfully," that's probably just the way it will be."

CHAPTER SEVEN

Sunlight sparkled through diamond-hung leaves and sprayed its aching blaze against Laine's throbbing head. He lay back against the pillows of the divan, watching Barclay's settled face.

Laine's lips pouted with a petulant fury. "I hand you a prime suspect on a steaming platter and you don't even blink your goddamned eyes."

"I'm stoical."

"Damned right you are."

"You're excitable."

"I got a lot of information last night in my excitement."

"Sure. And a bop on the head."

"That was because I wasn't watching."

"That's because you got upset when you saw the girl's name in the book."

Laine looked at the crumpled paper on the table by his side. "I have the evidence even if I was knocked cold."

"Sure. That was an accident. Like a dying man clutches at the blanket. Anyway, that's no evidence. It proves the girl was there, that's all."

Laine knew that was all. He searched around with mental tentacles for vindication of his pain. "If I hadn't been hit, I probably wouldn't have gotten my information."

"That's true." Barclay leaned forward. "How're you gonna use the information?"

"Why, hell, it puts Ten Eyck on the spot, doesn't it?"

"It gives him a motive. But how about the squealer?"

"The snow-snifter? Pop? Well, he's no good as a witness." Laine thought of the fawn-colored fingers groping in the air. "No. He's hardly reliable. But I think what he told me was the truth."

Barclay nodded. "What he said about the doctor fixing up a story about last night was true, too, and how he'd have the hospital in order."

Laine's face took on the blank look of thought. "His name-plate," he remarked dreamily," said 'Maurice X. Ten Eyck."

"So," said Barclay, "his middle name is X-Ray. I once knew a card sharp whose name was Decker and he pulled more aces off the bottom of the decker. And I knew another guy ...."

"This is different," said Laine coldly. "Ten means a lot of things to a lot of people. To some it means *commandments*. To others it means *probability*, such as a ten-to-one chance ... or maybe a decade. To Ten Eyck it's a name he's proud of and he points it up with the X initial-Roman numeral ten. It gives him a label." Laine looked at Barclay without expression. "Like what marked the girl's breast."

Barclay sat up straight. His face stiffened. "You shoulda hauled him in," he said.

Laine waved an airy hand. "He won't get away. I've sent some men out there. Got 'em posted. They've already reported in. Everything's quiet."

"Fast mover, aren't you?"

Laine grinned. "Don't know." He rubbed his head. "Sometimes, maybe." He lifted the telephone book from the table. A long pencil mark jagged across the page. "I think this is it, all right. Monkey-Monk out to Mockley. Dr. Gene Mockley. I figured I'd have to interpret it. The dope was a little garbled. Mockley's a big man with the moneyed set. I think it fits."

"Could be. How do we try it on for size?"

Laine's thought curled around possible plans. "We can't give him what we have. There's only enough to scare him off. We can't come right out and ask him who he peddled a baby for in 1951."

Laine decided. "We'll have to tell him just enough so he'll make a move."

"Fine," said Barclay. "Sounds difficult."

"I've got a facile tongue."

"Sure. But this is a man. The same oil you use on a woman won't work."

Laine stood, testing his head with small sideways motions.

"I checked that high school," Barclay offered.

Laine looked at him. "What'd you come up with?"

"I found out where the principal lived, so I went out there. She was hangin' Christmas cards on a long string around her walls. She's got a face like an axe and big square teeth and when I told her we found the school's telephone number on a corpse, she got all tingly and excited. All the time she talked about how awful it was, she was clackin' her teeth like she was sharpenin' 'em.

"She tried to link the Barnes girl up with everything from a freshman on the rolls to an old teacher that's fightin' off retirement." Barclay shook his head. "I was glad to get out of there. She was pretty sick when she had to tell me the school nurse was named Calaway instead of Conti."

"I'll bet," said Laine. He started for the door. "Well, let's get the trip to Mockley out of the way."

"Get an overcoat," suggested Barclay. "The sun's shining. But it's just shining light, not heat."

Lifting the coat from the closet, Laine allowed Barclay to help him shrug it on. "We'll take your car," said Laine, as they stepped from the apartment house, "and you drive."

"Head hurt?"

"Not too much. I just want to get its machinery in gear so I can handle this party. L. A. traffic might throw me off balance."

They headed out for the West Valley. Through the sprawling towns along the way, they passed under crossed branches of silver tinsel. "Like a couple of West Pointers getting married," observed Laine.

"Huh?"

"That tinsel. Like crossed sabres above our heads."

"Gotta start buyin' the kids' Christmas presents," said Barclay thoughtfully. "Junior wants a guitar so he can practice to be a cowboy on TV."

"Sensible."

"Billy wants a glass eye like that old magazine seller's got."

"What's Katherine want? A pair of gams like Betty Grable?"

"No. Katherine wants a baby sister."

Laine took a quick look at his companion. "What're you going to do about that?"

"We're gonna give it to her. But not 'til next June."

The houses were becoming larger and more remote, standing back from the street like aristocrats, pulling their skirts away from the common people. The estates were getting named, too, decorative signatures with a Spanish accent. They rolled to a stop before an aloof flagstoned wall.

"Should I drive in?" asked Barclay as he pointed out the grilled iron gate before the driveway.

"No," said Laine. "We'll be sneaky about this. You go around the block and park on the corner. I'll solo Mockley." He slammed the car door behind him.

Barclay raced the motor. "Keep your head outta the way," he warned as he drove off.

CHAPTER EIGHT

Laine stepped from the flagstoned terrace onto a rug that snuggled his ankles. The room, an oval bubble of light was semi-circled by cushioned chairs, upholstered to fit padded bodies, with arms that were now empty. The magazines, selected with care, as glossy as the table top where they lay, were carefully piled. The room was one to inspire confidence in the rich and make the poor know they were in the wrong place.

An arched opening framed the receptionist, her sweatered arms upraised as she fitted a saucy hat on a gamin haircut. Laine stepped to the window to watch with appreciation.

She whirled and dropped her arms. "Were you waiting for the doctor?"

"I was," said Laine, contemplative chin on the palm of his hand. "But that was then. This is now."

Her mouth tightened so that Laine knew immediately what she would look like in ten years.

"Office hours are over for the day. The doctor never takes patients other than by appointment."

"Independent."

"It's the usual office routine."

"I mean you. You're independent."

She slung a fur coat over her shoulders. She looked at Laine as if he were a shipment of defective vaccine. With finality, she closed the top part of the door and left him looking at the wooden panels. He grinned and made a silent bet with himself that had he worn a Brooks Brothers suit, she wouldn't have acted this way.

Laine walked softly toward a frosted glass door at the far end of the reception room. He reached out his fingers to tap them against it. The door cracked silently open. Pushing his head through, he gazed around a room which held a reclining lounge and an easy chair; an ivory portable radio on a small cream-colored chest stood close by. Laine took in the soothing color of the walls, the folded matching blanket at the end of the lounge. He stepped through and pushed open another door.

This cubicle was antiseptic white, the examination couch, pure and soft, upraised by chromium rods. It was surrounded by little cabinets which contained the methods for probing the inner man. Laine stood, his hands lightly resting against the sides of the door frame. There was something neurotic about the set-up. Too pat. Too soothing. He bet the doctor never talked above a whipped-cream monosyllable -like that soft murmur of conversation drifting in right now from somewhere beyond.

Laine crossed the tiles on the balls of his feet, and slowly, almost imperceptibly, turned the handle of the door. The murmur became more distinct, with occasional words clear. Laine pushed the door open to allow the crevice of a space and felt cold air seep through the crack.

The words became intelligible. "She's dead," said a man's voice, the quickness of impatience in it. "Why are you worried?"

The answer was threadlike with anxiety. "She threatened me. She was furious when I wouldn't let her see the baby. She said she'd do something. Something drastic."

"Well, she can't now. She's dead."

Unconsciously, Laine nodded with the finality of the statement.

"But there's a strange man around the place. He keeps going past. I'm scared of him. Maybe he's mixed up with her."

"It's your imagination. Go on home now and get some sleep. Here's a sedative."

Laine heard a rustle of movement, then a high voice, receding... "I'm glad she's dead..."

Counting to ten, he shoved open the door and stepped out onto a brick-floored patio, his attitude busy and important. His eyes, seemingly preoccupied, saw the red hair -the swish of a dress, as it crossed a strip of lawn and through an iron gate; saw the startled face of a man watching him—a doctor's white coat.

"What the devil are you doing here?"

Laine turned, to survey the surrounding. He looked then at the speaker. "You the owner here?" he asked importantly.

"I'm Dr. Mockley. Who are you?"

"I came to get your patio furniture." Laine whipped out a slip of paper from his pocket. It was his doodling page, covered with pencilled breasts, some round, some pendulous. "We got a call to reupholster it." Laine looked up brightly.

The girl had disappeared through a garden wall of the next property. Laine stroked the covering of a chaise longue. "Looks in pretty good condition to me."

"It is in good condition."

Laine looked at the doctor, whose face wasn't going along with this.

"Didn't you call the Laine Outdoor Furniture Repairers?"

"I did not."

"Well, I'll be...," Laine furrowed his brows in pseudo thought. "Whats the number here. 3118?"

"That's correct"

"3118 Palm Circle."

The doctor's face smoothed out. "No. This is Palm Drive."

"That's it." Laine snapped his fingers, folded the paper and jammed it into his pocket. "That fool driver can't read street signs. Well, sorry. Got to get over to Palm Circle." He turned to go through the suite of offices.

"Here. Out this way. "The doctor narrowed his eyes. "How did you get past the reception room?"

Laine hunched his shoulders. "Nobody there. Just walked through." He started down the walk.

"Don't forget," Dr. Mockley called, "tradesmen enter through the rear in this neighborhood."

"Caste system," grunted Laine.

CHAPTER NINE

"Well, you took long enough," grumbled Barclay as Laine got in the car.

"I called up at the drug store to have some men come out. I want 'em posted here."

Barclay started the motor. Laine reached over to switch it off. "Hold your horses. We'll wait for 'em. Keep your eyes peeled down the street. Don't want anyone getting itchy feet."

Barclay leaned back. "So you found out something."

"Yes." Laine smiled complacently. "You know who lives next to Mockley?"

"How many guesses do I get?"

"That's the Thurmond place. Name Thurmond mean anything to you?"

Barclay stroked his face. "Well, it sounds familiar. There's a market in my neighborhood called 'Thurmond Market!'"

"No relation. Remember the terms of the Thurmond will when Scottie Thurmond got killed in that crash-oh-'bout three years ago?"

Barclay drew his brows together. "Seems there was a mix-up, but I don't just exactly remember it."

"You don't remember it. Period," Laine grinned. "Stop pretending. Well, Scottie had this young wife who thought she was sitting on top of the world with an inheritance that would keep her there. Then came the will. It seems Scottie was living on the income of a trust fund, and should he die without issue, the principle was to go to a stepbrother..."

"What's an issue?"

"Oh, for God's sake, you've got three of 'em." Laine thought a moment. "Three and a half."

"You mean kids?"

"That's right."

"Then say kids."

"Okay. If Scottie should die without leaving any kids, the money was to go to a stepbrother. If Scottie had any kids, the trust fund was to go to them—which would make everything just dandy for the young wife."

"So?"

"Well, there weren't any kids."

Barclay whistled tonelessly.

"But," Laine hesitated for drama, "as soon as the will was read, the glamorous Mrs. Scottie Thurmond screams, 'But I *am* enceinte'."

"What's enceinte?"

"French for in the family way."

"Then say in the family way." Barclay settled back. "She was gonna have a kid after all."

"Maybe."

Barclay turned. "She said so."

"She said so."

"But she couldn't lie about it—" Barclay's face became more blank. "Oh, you mean she palmed off another baby?"

"Maybe."

"Mary Barnes' baby?"

"But how about the months—" Barclay squinted his eyes, remembering his wife's changing figure. "Well, how about that? Hey?"

Laine grinned. "She might have had Mockley swear she was pregnant. She could have gone away someplace."

"Yeah." Barclay weighed the problem.

"We'll check on it. Here come the boys."

A car slid up. Laine leaned out. "Watch Mockley's place and the Thurmond place next to it." Laine waved down the street. "The one with the flagstone wall and the hollow tile wall with the U drive. Watch for anyone acting suspicious. There might be a guy keeping his eyes on the Thurmond place. I want him. Tail anyone leaving either house."

Barclay started the car and they rolled on down the street.

"What fellow do you think is watching the Thurmond place?"

"I don't know," said Laine slowly. "But Mrs. Thurmond's worried about him. Mockley discounted him. But I'm not so sure." He turned to Barclay. "Anyone claim Mary Barnes' body yet?"

"Not yet."

They were silent as they passed back under the tinselled hangings over the busy streets, until Laine had a thought. "You say the woman next door to the Barnes girl in that hotel is sure of the radio?"

"Yeah." Barclay groaned. "What a dame! She was old enough to be my mother. Painted like a poster. I think she was what you called the Claridge kid the other day... a what?"

"A nympho?"

"Jeez, yes. I was scared I wouldn't get outta the place with my honor."

"But I'm sure you did. We'll have time yet today to check the back issues on this Thurmond lead.

CHAPTER TEN

The bare bulb gleamed down on the newsprint. The room smelled dusty.

"Don't they keep a fire going in this ice box?" growled Laine.

Barclay continued to read, his finger following the line of print.

"We've got it all, I think," said Laine. He spoke from his notes. "The will was read right after Scottie Thurmond was killed in December of '50. Mrs. Thurmond, on hearing the terms, announced the coming of an heir—or heiress. Then, dear kind Dr. Mockley jumped in to substantiate her claim by stating she had been under his care—and that little coup closely followed a big lawsuit against him which would probably have wiped him out…"

"But," interrupted Barclay, "Dr. Mockley was a wealthy man. It said so in the paper."

"Sure he was wealthy. Some of those wealthy ones, though, can't stand any extra-curricular expense. They're hanging by the skin of their teeth." Laine looked at Barclay. "You wouldn't understand that. You're just a salaried guy."

"What are you?"

"I'm another. But I know how the rich ones do. They get up to their necks in bills and spend all their income six months in advance. Mockley was ripe for a bribe. When it came, he clutched it.

"Pretty risky for Mockley."

"Oh, I guess he worried some. Then we see where Mrs. Thurmond drops from the society pages. Gone somewhere for her health. Neat, huh?"

"I suppose so. But I never would have taken the chance Mockley took."

"You'll never have the opportunity. Then they present the baby for the eyes of the attorney who read the will, and the eyes of the world—probably all fixed up with a fake birth certificate. Born July 10, 1951. A little girl. Mary Barnes went into the Parkway Hospital on the third. And she had a daughter. Check!" Laine stood up. "Come on. That night clerk ought to be on duty at the hotel. Let's talk to him."

Barclay heaved his bulk from the chair, groaning. "I talked to him. I talked to him twice already. Why again? He's as dumb as an ox. He don't know from nothing."

Barclay followed the smaller man out. "I don't want to get mixed up with that woman again."

"The painted job in the room next to the girl's?" asked Laine over his shoulder. "No. We won't fool around with her. She's hopeless."

"So's the clerk." They rolled slowly down the city streets, ablaze with light and decoration—busy with evening shoppers.

"I've gotta get some time off to buy the kids' Christmas presents," complained Barclay. "It's gettin' closer and closer."

"Maybe we'll get a bonus on this business if we clear it up and you can have a hell of a Christmas."

On every corner a Santa Claus rang his little bell. The store windows were confused movement with their mechanical displays, the traffic a tangle and impatient car horns a snarl. Barclay turned into a side street of pawn shops and taverns, turned again and drew up before the flickering sign which read 'ROOMS'.

"Have the police let the manager have his room back?" asked Laine.

"Yeah. We took all her stuff out and gave it up."

The clerk noted their entrance, the glassy eyes in his mouse face watchful. His liver-colored fingers with their dark tips tapped the desk top, an index to his shivering nerves. The few loungers in the lobby sprawled as if their spines had gone soft through the years.

Laine sniffed the chill dust of the air, borne down by the dampness of the building. He reached the desk, Barclay trailing, to lean against it, fastidiously holding his hands away from the stained wood.

"I want to ask you a few questions," said Laine "about the night of the murder."

"I been asked questions," whined the clerk. "I been asked and asked. I don't know nothin'."

"That I don't doubt," agreed Laine. "I thought maybe something might come to you if I suggested it."

"It always comes to him," broke in Barclay, "just as soon as you suggest it."

Laine leaned over the counter, his head held stiffly away as if there were an imaginary circle of quarantine about the clerk. "Now," he said soothingly, "did you see anybody go up the stairs or use the elevator on that night who didn't belong here? Someone, perhaps, who might be on a visit? Think carefully, someone who might have been carrying a portable radio?" He bounced back on his heels, looking brightly at the clerk. "A radio, see? Not many people carry radios around. You should remember that."

"I don't remember nothin'." The whine had become a sulky snarl. "Everybody looks alike. They're all carryin' somethin'. Why would I remember that?"

"Why, indeed," sighed Laine. His fingers drummed the desk top. Suddenly recollecting where they were, he lifted them and rubbed them against his coat. "Well, then, do you remember a man, tall, broad shouldered, good looking, well dressed, with black hair which grows to a peak in the middle of his forehead, on that night, carrying a radio?"

The clerk wrinkled his forehead, twisted his mouth. He narrowed his eyes, leaning his arms against the counter and looked off into nothing. "Yeah," he said slowly as if in a trance. "I kinda think I remember him. Tall, good lookin', black hair and carryin' a radio. I think so."

Barclay leaned forward. Laine watched the clerk closely—suspiciously. "Okay. Now, do you remember a man of average size, well dressed, curly grey hair, big nose, brown eyes—carrying a radio?"

The clerk fisted his hands in a spasm of concentration, the cords of his neck distended and his eyes became more glassy. "Grey hair, big nose. Yep. Carryin' a radio…"

Laine pursed his lips. "You're a good rememberer, aren't you?"

The clerk glowed with pride.

"All right," said Laine. "Now about a woman." He made semicircular motions in the air to indicate a well-rounded torso. "Built like a dream, with red hair … carrying a radio?"

The clerk's eyes heated with their thinking. His dirty fingernails scratched the surface of the desk. "Yeah. She was here. Red hair. Oh, boy!"

Laine whirled and started for the door. "Oh boy, is right," he growled. "A jughead if I ever saw one."

Out on the pavement, they found themselves in a cold drizzle. "High fog mixed with smog—or low smog mixed with fog," commented Barclay. "what were you tryin' in there, anyway?"

Laine laughed shortly. "The first one I described was Ten Eyck. The second, Dr. Mockley. The third was the best I could do on Mrs. Thurmond. God! What an imagination that clerk's got."

"He's a dummy."

CHAPTER ELEVEN

Laine jarred to his elbow, looked dazedly about. The whirr that awakened him sounded forth again. He yawned, reached over to jerk the telephone from its cradle.

"Okay. Okay. You got me awake. Now what do you want to do about it?" he said into the mouthpiece.

"Laine?" came Barclay's voice

"Sure. What is it?"

"Laine, they picked up the guy that was hanging around Thurmonds. Had a little trouble with him."

"Where is he now?"

"Down here at headquarters."

"You talked to him?"

"No. I just got here."

"Anybody talk to him?"

"Only routine stuff."

"Does he answer questions?"

"Well, yes and no."

"Okay. I'll come down. We'll go over him before the cops get to him."

"Come to the morgue. We're gonna take him down there."

"Why?"

"To see if he knows the girl."

"Okay. See you there." Laine clicked the telephone back into position and padded to the kitchen. He started his coffee, took a glass of orange juice from the refrigerator and gulped it. While the coffee bubbled, sending flat waves of hot scent through the apartment, Laine dressed. He stared out the window. The sun didn't look as if it would shine today. Maybe the rainy season would hold its grip.

The coffee made him feel good, bringing him wide awake, so that, as he drove down the boulevard, his mind seemed to be clicking. His head felt like his own again. He was glad to have it back.

The Hall of Records looked like an old hag with the smog a shawl around her shoulders. The City Hall a stately showgirl after a hard night. He wedged his coupe between two fog-misted sedans and leaped down the stairs to the morgue.

Barclay bulged against an inner door, his face as placid as if he had nothing more important to think about than the weather. Two uniformed policemen stood on each side of the prisoner. Laine watched the slouching figure between them.

There was a sharpness to the man's face—sadism battling with the saint. The smooth, half-planed cheeks ended in shadowy jaws, unsure whether they would settle or remain always undecided. The mouth had made up its mind. It had thinned and twisted into discontent.

The clothes were a detriment, but gave the air of being shabby not from poverty, but through insensibility—as if the wearer thought of them with indifference. At last the man looked up and Laine came in contact with the eyes of a zealot.

"What's your name?" he asked, waiting while the eyes expressed nothing. Laine turned toward Barclay, who hunched his shoulders and spread his hands. "Some questions he answers. Some, he don't."

Laine jerked his hand toward the door. Barclay leaned against it to push it open and walked through. Laine motioned the prisoner and his keepers. He brought up the rear, tugging the collar of his coat about his neck as the chill air struck him.

Barclay was standing by the sheeted mound; white dune of anonymity. Laine walked around to stand next to him, looking over the bleached hillock into the paradoxical face across the slab. He almost caught a quick ripple of the jaw. His eyes flicked upward at the window above where a sick line of yellow light escaped through the clouds. He wondered if it were the play of the sunbeam which caused the wave of motion, or if it were a tensing of the nerves, a jamming together of teeth in preparation of what was to come.

Barclay plucked the sheet back and a still, waxen mask lay there sleeping. Laine stared at features which were beautiful now that serenity had been moulded there in place of protesting distortion.

The cloud of hair appeared alive, a fine spray of it lifting to settle again at a quick puff of air from one of the watchers. Laine looked up. The prisoner's face was cataleptic. Had it moved, Laine must have missed the motion during his absorption of the dead.

The man was gazing now, not at the still features, but at the stiff shroud. A policeman shuffled his feet, teeth chattering. Barclay twitched the sheet, wanting to put its protective layers again in place.

"You know her?" Laine's voice cracked like a discord above the bier.

"No." The answer was soft, but it screamed through the eyes.

"Certain?" Laine looked from the brows of the corpse to the brows of the living, and saw there the same flaring tips, the same uprise toward the temples.

"I deny a sinner."

Laine's sudden knowledge traveled from the dead girl to the living disclaimer. "She was your sister?"

Barclay stared from the slab to the prisoner. His fingers jerked the sheet back over the still features as if this were a station stop on the girl's long journey.

"I protest relationship to a transgressor. I repudiate the blood in her veins as being the same as mine ..."

"She hasn't got any blood—now," Laine barked. He smoothed the sheet tidily and walked around the slab. "When she had some, it carried the same pedigree as yours." He pulled a notebook from his pocket. "What's your name?"

"I remain without identity. The name has now been smirched."

"Oh, hell." Laine turned to the policemen. "Take him away. Lock him up on a vag charge. Let him cool off for awhile. I'll get to him later. Book him under the name of Barnes."

CHAPTER TWELVE

The outer door closed behind the policemen with their charge. Barclay lounged against the wall. Laine slouched on the edge of the table. He rubbed his hands together. "Damned cold in there."

"They did look alike," said Barclay.

"Sure they did. I didn't catch it right away. Wasn't thinking along those lines." He gave his palms a final massage, turned his coat collar down… "I wonder what it means?" he asked softly.

"It could mean," suggested Barclay, "that he fixed the girl good, he with his nutty ideas."

"Yes," said Laine, "castigation—his cock-eyed form of retribution." Then he pounded the table with an angry fist and stood straight. "As far as I'm concerned, this guy just louses up the case. Ten Eyck is my choice. I don't want any other suspect horning in."

"You just want to get Ten Eyck for that bop on your head."

"Maybe." Laine's eyes were lukewarm as they rested on his co-worker. "Right now, I want to go and talk to Mrs. Thurmond. She know you picked up this character in front of her house?"

"No. She don't even know we got the boys stationed around there. She don't know from nothin'."

"Good. What was he doing? Just prowling around?"

"Who? Barnes?"

Laine grinned. "He wants to remain without identity. Remember?"

"Yeah. Without identity. He walked back and forth a few times early this morning. About dawn. Then he left. He didn't know it, but he had a tail on him. The tail said he just wandered around without rhyme or reason. He was quite a walker. The tail's tired. Then he come back to the house and paced, so they grabbed him."

Laine started for the door. "You going with me to the Thurmonds?" he asked over his shoulder.

"Don't think so." Barclay lounged after him.

"Gotta make a report. When do you want to talk to the guy? How long you think he ought to cool off in his cell?"

Laine glanced at his watch. "Make it after lunch. About one-thirty. I'll meet you there."

The tinkling of Santa Claus bells made an overtone of chuckling mirth through the misty city streets, the decorations an eye-confusing kaleidoscope. Laine headed out toward the Valley and west. The deodars on green residential lawns splashed crimson and silver with their trim. Nostalgic Easterners had whitewashed the corners of their windowpanes in simulated drifted snow. Poinsettias stretched scarlet fingers in hedgerows and wreaths looked like frosted doughnut rings on doorways.

Laine slowed his car before the Thurmond estate. The house, its sheets of plate glass weeping in the drizzle, the lazy drift of smoke from the fireplace chimney curling low, stood on a broad velvet terrace. Laine stepped out. The car on the corner was official. The car in the center of the block was official. But only he knew it. He pushed open the ornate gate and walked through.

"Who shall I say is calling?" asked the maid at the door.

"Tell her Inspector Laine."

The maid became dignified with overlapping edges of condescension. "Perhaps you should have gone to the back. One of the servants could have talked to you. What is it you're inspecting?"

"Well, it's not gas meters," said Laine impatiently. "I'm from the Sheriff's Office. I want to see Mrs. Thurmond. Get her."

A small child sidled into the entrance hall from another doorway. She looked to be three or four. A fairy child.

He stooped. "Hello."

The child looked up at him gravely. The dark angel's wings above her eyes with their rising tips gave contrast to her face. The slanted brows held him staring.

"Susan, go to your room." The voice which turned him was only partly sharp—the rest of the edge was fear. The child stood to finish her contemplation, then with indifference, because this stranger had nothing to do with her, she left the room.

"Your daughter?" Now he took in the red hair and the creamy skin. The woman inclined her head. A peasant and harlot were deftly joined to make her face. Money had given her her manner.

"I'm Inspector Laine from the Sheriff's Office."

She led him through an archway and waved him to an easy chair. The flames of the fireplace licked out, held back only by the golden links of the curtain before it. The blaze made the woman's hair more glowing, and kindled her face into something feverish. Laine leaned forward. She might be hard to handle. Her kind was dynamite. He liked them that way.

He lit a cigarette and through the smoke, asked his questions. "Have you noticed a prowler around your property recently—or, let us say, someone who seemed interested in the place or something in it?"

"No," she said, but her involuntary start gave truth to the words he had heard her speak to Dr. Mockley. "No. Why?"

"We picked one up. We don't know what he wanted. We thought you might tell us."

"No. I don't know what he wanted. How would I know? Maybe he wanted to steal something."

"Maybe." Laine flicked his ashes into a bronze tray big enough for a foot bath. "Maybe he just wanted to look at something. Or hurt something."

"How silly." The redhead rose and walked to the fire. She spread her hands before its flame.

"Maybe he likes children. Or maybe he doesn't like children. You've got a pretty little girl."

She whirled, staring at him. Two quick lines passed down the woman's cheeks, a picture of her future in ten years.

"She does look like a dead woman I saw, though."

The woman's eyes turned from him. He followed their gaze. The child was walking softly toward him, a small box in her arms, a cobalt plastic box with a handle on top.

"Susan, go to your room."

Laine stretched out a hand. "What do you have there, honey? Let's see it." He was looking at her winged brows.

Then he really saw the box, with its little round speaker, its slatted grooves. "A radio," he said with a quick downthrust of his lips, a glance at the woman before the fireplace. "A lovely, lovely radio."

"Mama bought it," said the child. She placed the box on Laine's lap. "Mama bought it for Susan." She patted the box. "Susan's radio."

Laine twisted a knob and a soft Christmas Carol drifted into the room. He snapped it silent. "A nice little battery set. When did Mama buy it?"

"Oh, a little while." The child clutched the box again and sidled off.

"When did you buy it, Mrs. Thurmond?" Laine stood up, crushed out his cigarette and watched the woman.

"I don't know. A week ago, maybe two weeks. What does it matter?"

"Perhaps it matters a lot. Perhaps it doesn't matter at all." Laine stepped close to her. He could smell her and she smelled good, like dew-wet violets or freshly opened lilacs. It was a surprise, the heavy scent of gardenias was her type—sultry. He brought back his thoughts and found the woman staring at him, narroweyed, a little inviting.

Laine jerked his coat more firmly on his shoulders. "You might be in for a lot of trouble, Mrs. Thurmond. I'll tell you now, your house is being watched. Don't leave it." He caught the fresh garden scent again as he moved close. He held his breath. "Mrs. Thurmond," he said, "I think you're as guilty as hell."

CHAPTER THIRTEEN

The drizzle had evaporated in the rays of the sun that shone down between two black clouds. The pavement steamed and Laine draped his topcoat on the back of the car seat when he got out to walk up the steps.

Barclay sat on a stone ledge in front of the building. "Maybe we'll have a bright Christmas," he said.

"Maybe." Laine tossed his cigarette and watched it sizzle out in a puddle on the grass.

"How was Mrs. Thurmond?"

Laine rolled his eyes. "Mrs. Thurmond is a vanilla sundae topped with strawberries. Mrs. Thurmond is a creamy rose with red-tipped petals…"

"Hm. I knew I shoulda gone. You're a push-over. See the kid?" '

"I saw her." Laine pushed open the double doors and Barclay followed him in. "She looks just like her mother."

"You mean Mrs. Thurmond?"

"The girl in the morgue." Laine turned and stopped on his way down the corridor. "She's got the same eyebrows Mary Barnes has. The same eyebrows that guy's got we're going to see. Have you talked to him?"

Barclay shook his head. "I stopped at the desk and looked over the stuff they checked before they stuck him in the jug."

"Yeah? What'd he have on him?"

Barclay ticked off the items on his fingers. "He had a coin purse in his pocket with thirty cents in it, a dirty handkerchief, and a curved hunk of ivory about two inches long, all carved like a totem pole. The desk sergeant said it was a good luck charm." Barclay looked at Laine for confirmation. "Probably made out of a polar bear's tooth."

"Could be," agreed Laine, nodding.

"He had a little brass cross, too. He blew his top when they lifted that. Said nobody should separate a man from his crucifix." Barclay stroked his chin thoughtfully. "I never saw one like it before. You know how the long part usually sticks up above the top piece?" He illustrated by forming a cross of his two forefingers.

Laine nodded, watching closely.

"Well, this one wasn't made that way. That top part was a ring..."

Laine started to grin.

"You ever see one like that?"

"I've seen pictures of them." Laine chuckled as he started walking again down the corridor. "Barnes didn't have to go into a religious seizure over that. It's no Christian cross. It's a phallic symbol."

"Huh?" Barclay peered at him.

"Originally, it was the Egyptian emblem of life. The priests carried it. It's been handed down through history. Not by the Christians, though."

"He had this, too." Barclay fished in his pocket and came up with a slip of paper.

Laine stared. "I'll be damned. The Hanover number again."

"Yeah. And see what else."

"It says Judas Iscariot." Laine took the sheet and crumpled it into his pocket.

"Nobody over at the school named that," said Barclay.

"No," said Laine. "It's like the cross. A symbol. We'll take a trip to the Valley and see if we can dig up something."

They walked between the cells and through catcalls and jeers, their faces expressionless. Now they were officers of the law and granite. Barclay jerked his head at the turnkey, who jingled his way before them. Laine peered through the bars at the stoic on the cot. The turnkey pushed open the door. The steel door clattered behind them.

"Well, Barnes," said Laine, and the man on the cot raised his head.

The shadow of a smile lined Laine's lips. He crossed over to sit on the cot in cozy nearness. Barclay straddled a wooden chair.

"Let's have your story about why you were hanging around the Thurmond place," said Laine.

"Walking," said the prisoner. "Just walking and thinking."

Laine clasped his hands loosely between his knees. "Well, a man's got a right to walk and think." He waited while the silence grew long and heavy. "Of course," he qualified, "it might depend a little on where he's walking and what he's thinking about."

Again the shroud of quiet. Laine leaned over to tap the other on the arm. The prisoner drew from him as if the touch were a contamination.

"You were looking for the child, weren't you? You were looking for your sister Mary's baby."

Laine stared into the masklike face with its clamped lips. "What were you planning to do with the child? Your niece?"

"I deny…"

"To hell with your denunciations. Who are you to go around denying things? Who are you to try to take the law into your hands? Be the judge and the jury… where were you last Monday night at 11:30?"

"Walking. Just walking—through shadowed valleys—for the fleshpots hold the food of evil—" The voice which began as a whisper, rose.

"A fleshpot or two might be a good thing for you. Where were you last Monday night at 11:30?"

Walking. Just walking through righteous paths—"

"Where'd they take you? Right up to a fourth-class hotel to your sister's room?"

"Hotels are bad places."

"Yeah," grunted Laine. "There are people in 'em. Do you have a radio?"

"Radios are instruments of the devil. They bring songs of lust—thoughts of depravity—"

Laine watched him closely. "You might be right, at that. Did you kill your sister?"

"What kills woman is her own sin which festers and grows until the cancer eats into—"

Laine looked away, then leaned toward the prisoner, his lips lifting away from fanged incisors as if to cut the words at him, but they came out carefully gentle. "Where do you live, Barnes?"

"In a cloister of my own."

Laine's mouth became a thin line, a dash between disgust and violent temper.

Barclay rocked on two legs of his chair. "Where is this cloister?"

The prisoner pointed to his heart.

"Like a turtle," said Laine. "He carries his home with him." He turned a shoulder toward the prisoner. "You thought your sister was a bad girl?"

The prisoner sat very still. Only his eyes seemed alive. His lips were as stiff as a ventriloquist's. "We are born in sin. She who would add foulness to the calumny shall bear only stigmata to be perpetuated as a plague."

"In English, you're saying your sister bore this child out of wedlock."

"I have no sister—"

Laine jerked himself from the cot, his face twisted with fury and frustration. He motioned the turnkey. Barclay followed him out and down the corridor.

"You get so mad, Laine," he complained. "If you just wouldn't get so mad."

Laine took a cigarette from his package and struck the match savagely. "Well, the damn fool talks in riddles. In parable, maybe. I can't stand it. If he won't talk sense, I won't fool around."

"Well, then, who's gonna fool around?"

"You do it. Or let one of the boys do it."

"Now, Laine—you know how the boys do. I didn't think you liked rough stuff."

"Listen—" They were at the outer door now, in the main hall-way. "Listen, Barclay, have a call issued from all radio stations contacting anyone who might know that Barnes and where he lives. And have news items placed in all the newspapers. The big ones and the little sheets through the Valley."

"Yeah?"

"I want to see that character's room. I want to talk to his friends if he's got any." Laine became thoughtful. "This is Friday. Keep it hot until Sunday. If nothing turns up by then, we'll let him go and follow him."

"It might work."

"I hope the publicity does the business. I don't want to let him loose."

"That guy oughtta be behind some kinda bars." Barclay's deadpan became over-serious. "Maybe we oughtta send him down to the beer tavern."

"What in hell for?"

"To have 'em put a new head on him."

CHAPTER FOURTEEN

Laine leaned across the greasy desk. "You see," he explained to the two teeth in the pinched mouth, "we have to have something to go on. It's impossible that you saw everybody in the case stomping up to the murdered girl's room. It just isn't logical."

The mouse face was intent upon every word.

"We've run into another fellow who has a kind of gruesome outlook. I'm going to describe him to you." Laine found himself speaking slowly, accenting his syllables. "If you don't think you saw him, or if you're not sure you saw him, come right out and say so, it'll be all right. But if you did see him, tell me so, and for God's sake, concentrate!"

"With a radio in his hand?" suggested the clerk helpfully.

"That's right. With a radio in his hand. Or maybe the radio was wrapped up in paper so no one would know it was a radio."

The lips passed over long front teeth, then they parted.

"The man's probably about twenty-six or seven, but he looks older."

This was difficult. Laine waited for it to absorb.

"His hair is thin and sandy. He's about—oh, he's about your height, narrow shouldered, slim, and his face is …" Laine raised his hands in the air, making little half-hearted gestures, trying to describe the nebulous cruelty of the face, and its fanaticism, "thin," he finished, "with shining eyes."

Laine frowned when he had completed the description. He looked about the lobby with its slouching hangers-on. His verbal sketch would fit most of them. He grunted, his nose wrinkling with remote distate.

The mouse face brightened, glowed, "I seen him," he said with excitement. "Sure. I seen that guy."

Laine stretched his lips into a gash, his eyes showing disgust.

"But there wasn't no package under his arm. It was a box. A wooden box." The clerk looked up for approval.

Laine leaned over, trying to read truth and reliability in the face. He shrugged. "Okay," he said tonelessly and left the hotel. The street was still and clear, the night air almost balmy. His car, parked at the curbing, presented no escape for his problem-tangled mind. A passerby wove gently down the sidewalk, humming the toneless tune carrying a lilt of cheer, the feet performing an involuntary ballet.

A beer sign, with its uncertain on-and-off flicker, caught Laine's eye. From the door, the bad breath of its interior spewed forth. No cocktail lounge this, with its video come-along, but a place for battered escapists to compete with a popping radio.

Laine leaned against a stool and as he motioned the bartender, he heard the last of the broadcast appeal: "If you should know the man of this description, or know where he lives, the Los Angeles Police request that you get in immediate touch with headquarters."

Laine lifted the mug and drank his beer to the opening bars of distorted jazz. A tug at his coat sleeve brought his gaze down into ale-colored, pink rimmed eyes. "That guy, Barnes," mouthed the relaxed lips. "He's a slick one." The eyes turned stupidly crafty. "I know where he holes in."

Laine pushed the mug back, looking carefully at the speaker. "You do?" he asked softly.

"Sure. I ain't gonna tell."

"The hell you aren't," said Laine. He laid a bill on the counter, pressing it down tidily, nodded to the bartender, and lifted his companion from the stool with a firm grip on his shoulder. The racket and confusion of the tavern continued.

"Here. Cut it out—" protested the drunk.

Laine propelled him from the bar and into the street. "Now," he said, "lead me to it."

"To what?" The whine had a snarl around its edges.

"The place where Barnes lives."

"You can't make me."

"The hell I can't." Laine jerked the man from his feet, dangled him a moment and set him down again.

"You a cop?" The face twisted like a small, repulsive child's, its whimper on the verge of tears.

"I'm a cop. Get going. Where does he live?" Laine drew in his breath slowly, expelling it in cautious little jerks.

"I'll show you." The man's body shook in time with his voice. "It's down the street here."

Laine walked beside the intricate steps of his guide. They reached the shadowy building which neighbored the hotel.

Laine's mouth slowly dropped open. He looked once upon the familiar sick sign indicating ROOMS next door. His eyes grew hard as he plunged in after the fumbling shuffle. The steps were in half-light to show their cavernous centers of numerous footprints. As the preceding drunk held to the bannister, it bent with his erratic weight. Laine was close upon his shuffling heels. At the head of the stairway, the drunk pushed through a door to stand blinking in the light of the room.

Laine followed him in. His eyes shifted to the iron bed in the corner. In its valley lay a pallid bulk of man, a bottle on the mountainous belly, the red-rimmed eyes placidly surveying his guests.

"When'd you get out?" blurted the drunk.

"Is this Barnes?" said Laine.

The drunk's sway held a moment as he nodded.

The prone man smiled lazily. "Yeah. What about it? I done my hitch. Now I wanna be alone." The small eyes, sunk in their fleshy bags, narrowed.

Laine turned toward the drunk. His words bit off, "You damn fool idiot." Then he groaned, "just when I thought I had something." Suddenly, his hands shook. He could feel anger wash over him like a scalding spray. He reached out a quick fist and caught the drunk under the chin. Quietly, the drunk settled to the floor, his listing legs becalmed, his restless hands tranquil, his face blissful in a pleasant dream.

Laine heard laughter from the bed, an unhealthy mirth. His fist grazed over the hand clutching its bottle on the mound of jarring flesh. Rivulets of liquid spouted forth from the neck of the bottle—a capricious geyser on the agitated paunch.

CHAPTER FIFTEEN

Laine's metabolism regained its balance with the rhythm of the engine. He smiled at the absurd scene in which he had just played the straight man's role. He was driving through a modest residential district, one of small homes and tidy lawns. Turning into an orderly driveway, he parked under a pepper tree.

Before the door of the bungalow opened, he could hear the sounds of family life within, like a warm and regular heartbeat. In another breath, it was all about him.

He laughed. "Hi kids," he greeted, trying to free his legs from grasping hands.

Mrs. Barclay smiled. She looked closely into Laine's face. "Come away, children. It's past your bedtime, and I think Mr. Laine wants to talk with daddy."

Laine gave her a little nod and followed Barclay into his den. It was a tiny room. Barclay closed the door, the clamor of the children became a murmur.

Laine pulled out a cigarette. He sighed and relaxed in a leather chair. "Have you had anything on the broadcasts or news items yet?" he asked as he struck a match and leaned back.

Barclay grunted, letting himself down carefully. "Nothing genuine," he said, "We've heard from all the crackpots in town. Publicity hounds keep us busy checking, and the usual idiots."

"But no leads?"

"Nothing legit."

"Well, I just ran down a hair-brained back alley and got my leg pulled." Laine laughed wrily and snubbed out his cigarette.

"Some drunk in a tavern down close to that hotel led me on a chase. I knocked him to sleep for it."

Barclay shook his head. "That temper of yours."

"He said he knew where Barnes lived. So I armed him out of the beer joint and made him lead me to the place. It was right next door to the hotel."

Barclay sat straight to look interested.

"Sure," agreed Laine, "that's how I felt. I figured maybe Barnes had rented a room next door and made his plans. But it was a bust."

Laine's face writhed as his memory recalled the pale hunk on the bed. "This Barnes was already in the room. Just got out of the pokey, I figured. He was as big as his name—and after the description on the radio! What a bunch of palookas run around loose."

"He made one outta you, huh?"

Laine pinched his lower lip sullenly. "I suppose he did." He grew thoughtful. "I guess," he concluded slowly, "it's about time to leave off tiptoeing. I think we'd better start tramping on a few feelings."

"Meaning whose?"

"First, meaning Dr. Ten Eyck's."

"You didn't tiptoe around him. You just didn't duck fast enough. You been mutterin' and lickin' your wounds ever since."

"I could have had the boys haul him in for questioning. I could have had 'em question everybody on the place."

"For what?"

"To find out where he was last Monday."

"Sure. Sure you could have. We haven't got proof he's runnin' a racket. What little we have got's got such big loopholes in it, he could slide through like nothin'. If we questioned him, and we were wrong, he could raise a pretty stink." Barclay shook his head.

"There's Pop. He knows the joint's a phony."

"The coke snifter? What kind of a witness would he be? Anyway, I bet he wouldn't come through."

Laine knew he wouldn't. "Well, I'm going to clamp down on Ten Eyck anyway. I'm going to turn that place upside down. I'll find evidence enough to keep him where I want him when this thing breaks."

"You don't think he'll have evidence you can touch, do you? You don't think he leaves stuff layin' around so we can fan his face with it, do you?"

"I don't know. I'll find out." Laine thought a few moments. "Then there's Mrs. Thurmond. A woman would be strong enough to wind a pillowcase around a girl's neck, especially if she sees a trust fund flapping away from her—and if she's scared she might not catch up with it. That would give her strength. Where was she Monday night?"

Barclay shrugged. "I can't see her fixin' up the girl with an 'X marks the spot'. You can ask her, though. But she's dynamite, too. A pair of eyebrows isn't enough to go on, and a rich dame like her could scream 'frame-up'. Why, every slick lawyer in town would help her."

Laine's face became stubborn. "Okay. I'll give 'em the chance. I'll also give Mockley a chance to pull a few wires." Laine stood. "I'm going to find out where everybody in this goddamned case was last Monday. I'm going to wring it out of them. If I'm wrong, and things go haywire, well then—I'll get me a job in a grocery store."

CHAPTER SIXTEEN

Laine tapped his fingers on the steering wheel in time to the idle of the engine. He stared belligerently through the fan of vision made clear by the windshield wiper. "What in hell's holding things up?"

Barclay was relaxed, his hands folded over his paunch. "It's an accident up ahead, I think. This line's going forward a little—"

"Damn little," said Laine, shifting into low and gaining a foot.

"An accident, I'll bet. The only time I ever saw the entrance to Cahuenga Pass like this was for the Santa Claus Parade."

"Maybe this's it."

"It's next week. I want to take my kids if I'm not still tied up."

A tow truck blasted its horn and pushed in through the wrong-way traffic, its red flasher reflecting red rain drops.

"I'll bet it's a bad accident." Barclay rolled down the window and leaned out.

"You'll get water on the brain out there," observed Laine. "It's coming down in bucketsful."

Barclay settled back and closed the window. "I guess it's right in front of the pink convertible."

Laine looked into his rear view mirror. "If I wasn't all hemmed in here, I'd take one of the cross streets and circle around Riverside Drive."

"We'll be out in a minute." Barclay, at ease, watched the Valley traffic come off the pass and into Hollywood.

"It's tough driving during the Christmas buying season. I wish I owned a store right now. I'll bet if I owned a store that handled ties and socks and handkerchiefs, I'd make a mint right now. Or a store that sold toys—"

"I wish I was a grocery clerk," said Laine, "or that I was a milkman or something—"

The line of traffic surged forward. Laine sat up straight and pressed down on the accelerator. "Boy," he said, "here we go. I always figure if a wheel rolled off my car or the rear end fell out, it'd happen right here on the pass where people drive like maniacs."

Barclay pointed. "Yeah. That's where it was." He waved at a policeman who was just climbing into his patrol car. "I wonder if anyone was killed?"

"I doubt it," said Laine. "It probably just pushed some dumb uninsured cluck into the hospital and spoiled his family's Christmas." The rain streamed down and the passing cars on each side of them sounded like the tide going out.

They left the freeway and turned to their right toward Burbank. "You'll have to direct me, now," said Laine, "you know where this woman lives."

Barclay leaned forward to watch the street signs. When they drove up in front of the stucco duplex, the rain had gathered momentum. They made a run for the small front porch. Laine leaned against the buzzer. "I hope she's home," he said.

"She's home. I called her. She's probably worn a hole in the carpet by now."

The woman stood there, smiling, her short upper lip drawn free of her large, square teeth. Her mouse-colored hair, grey-streaked, was cut short and curled into stubby ends, it's fine locks barely covering her skull. She drew the door wide, her eyes glinting sparks of welcome.

"Miss Gillam," said Barclay, formally correct, "this is Inspector Laine from the Sheriff's Office. He wants to ask you some questions." Barclay walked into the small living room, then, and stared at the Christmas cards suspended on a length of narrow red ribbon along one wall. They looked like intimate washing hung up to dry.

Crocheting her fingers into a tight pattern, Miss Gillam led Laine to an easy chair. She sat opposite, erect and stiff on the edge of a springless divan.

"That poor girl. The gentleman—" she gestured vaguely toward Barclay who stood moodily contemplating the colorful cards, his hands loosely clasped behind his back, "the gentleman who's with you told me about the poor thing the other day— and how she had the school's number among her—effects. How strange!" Sucking her upper lip against her teeth, she leaned forward stiffly, "what do you suppose it means?"

Laine glanced away from the light in her eyes. "Are there any men teachers on your staff, Miss Gillam?"

"Men? Why yes," she said with pleased lines around her mouth, "we do have several—do you think?—then she drew back coyly, and offered, "There's Mr. Armstrong who teaches Science—" Laine whipped out his notebook and an automatic pencil. Writing rapidly, he watched her as she stared at the ceiling, reciting the names.

"—Mr. Riley, our English teacher. The football coach is Mr. Paxton. Mr. Turnbull has the Algebra and Geometry classes and Mr. Wisecarver is our new Latin teacher." Her eyes left an imaginary list on the ceiling and rested on Laine. "That's all," she finished.

Thoughtfully, Laine looked down at his book. Tiring of the Christmas cards, Barclay had strolled to the window to stare through the stiff glass curtains at the pelting rain outside.

"I want to see them," said Laine, flicking the paper with his fingernail.

Miss Gillam gave an eager invitation. "I'm having a little Christmas get-together for the staff—"

Laine shook his head.

"—tomorrow night. It might be a good idea if you could come along and mingle with the guests."

"No," disagreed Laine flatly. "That wouldn't be a good idea."

"I wouldn't tell them who you were," she fluttered, "you could search for clues—"

Laine leaned forward. "Miss Gillam, we don't suspect this—" He glanced down at his writing. "This Riley or Wisecarver or whatchamacallit—we're just following leads for information. You run and get me a list of addresses and you won't have to worry about anything."

Miss Gillam left the room. When she returned with the list, she was sulky.

"Are all these men in town during the holidays?"

"All but Mr. Paxton."

"The coach?"

"He's up north somewhere."

Laine stood. "I want to thank you, Miss Gillam, for your very valuable assistance."

"Not at all. If there's anything more I can do. Anything at all—"

"We'll call on you," finished Laine. At the door, he said, "this is a routine investigation. The telephone number might mean nothing more important than that the girl wanted to enroll in night school."

Miss Gillam's face fell. "That's right," she said at the indigestible idea. "It might."

"And probably does." Laine opened the door, bowed slightly and stepped to the porch.

He and Barclay ran through the rain for the curb where the car was parked. Inside, Barclay said, "Maybe it does mean the girl wanted to enroll in night classes."

"With the same telephone number written along with the words 'Judas Iscariot' in Barnes' pocket?" scoffed Laine.

"Oh, yeah." Barclay watched thoughtfully while Laine stepped on the starter. "Why pick on teachers?" he wondered, "maybe it's some pupil—a young Peeping Tom or a yackin' kid who tells tales outta school—" Barclay turned, bright-eyed.

The car gained momentum. "No," Laine discounted with emphasis. "Boys are little devils. They don't get labelled Judases until they get bigger."

They found Wisecarver out in the rain, pruning roses. He smiled at them, the rain dripping off his rubber hat brim in a veil around his pleasant face.

After he had dropped his raincoat and hat on the service porch and led them into his compact, tiled kitchen, he listened while he warmed up the coffee. "Mary Barnes?" he asked, turning his pale blue eyes on them. "No. I can't say I remember knowing anyone by the name of Barnes since I was in Iowa. And that, gentlemen," he twinkled, "has been well over twenty-five years ago."

Unconcerned with their questions, he led them, coffee cup in hand, around the kitchen, pointing out the plants on the windowsills, and calling them by Latin terms like a fond parent who abhors nicknames.

"No," he repeated, "I don't even remember hearing the name." He touched a violet with a delicate forefinger. "Of course," he smiled, "about the only times I talk with my fellow teachers are at lunch or during meetings, and then we usually discuss the wickedness of the younger generation, rather than the charm of women friends."

"Well," said Laine at last, "thanks for the coffee." He set his cup on the table. "We'll be shoving off, now, and we're sorry we interrupted your pruning."

"No bother, gentlemen. If I do come in contact with a Miss Mary Barnes, I shall surely let your department know about it."

"You do that," said Laine soberly.

"Nice old boy," observed Barclay in the car. "We can strike him off the list." Barclay held the notebook high in the early twilight of the afternoon.

"Riley lives out in the Riverside Ranchos. That's not far from here."

They traveled a few blocks and Laine turned off the windshield-wiper. "Looks like the rain's over for a while."

"Yeah," said Barclay. "There's a sunbeam—there's always enough sun, even if it's for a minute, to prove the Chamber of Commerce is right when it says the sun shines 366 days out of the year in California."

No one was home at the small, glossy ranch-type bungalow.

Laine slumped behind the wheel of the car. "Who's left?" he asked.

"Armstrong and Turnbull," said Barclay, peering at the list. "Turnbull lives over on Shadynook. That's not far away. He's the one that teaches—"

"Mathematics?"

Laine turned on the lights to cut the optical difficulty of the evening haze. The beams shimmered weakly over wet streets. "I hope we get finished with this before it really gets dark," he sighed, "I hate to look for numbers by flashlight. I feel as guilty as if I were on the other side of the fence."

"This's Shadynook. The even numbers are on my side. Whoa. I think this is it."

They stepped out onto wet grass, found the flagged path and walked up the terrace. Barclay pushed the button and the door opened up on a beer bottle of a man, wide from the hips down.

"Your name Turnbull?" asked Laine.

"He's a tenant. Lives in our guest house at the rear. Go around this way." He trundled out to point. "There's the wooden gate. It's got one of those pull latches on it. I think I saw him come home a little while ago."

"This is a nice place," Laine said as he walked by the side of the hedge and unlatched the gate. "If I could find a cute girl with a lot of snap who hadn't been too much pawed over by guys like me, I'd get married and have a place like this."

"You couldn't afford it," said Barclay, "not on your pay. I got a house half as nice as this and it keeps me broke. It and my wife and my three kids and the one that's comin'—"

The cottage was small and silvery. A flicker of firelight shone through the front studio window. Laine tapped the large brass knocker.

The young man who answered the door appeared owlish in his dark rimmed glasses. He had a firm chin, clefted to give it a look of delicacy. He carried a book in his hand with a forefinger marking his place. Raising his brows in question, the glasses slipped forward a fraction.

"Mr. Turnbull?" asked Laine.

"Yes." His voice was soft, but the word was clipped.

Laine stepped inside, followed by Barclay. He snapped the door behind him. Turnbull looked a little surprised.

"We're detectives," explained Laine. He noted the precision of magazines laid fanwise on a large, square coffee table.

"Why me?" asked Turnbull.

Laine shrugged and sat down in an easy chair. He spread his hands to the fire. "A long shot that you might know the answers."

Turnbull backed in front of the blaze. His body became a silhouette and the soft lamplight just missed his face. Two of the magazines, Laine noted, were popular men's publications. One was a mathematical puzzle book. The rest were news-weeklies. Barclay sat down in the matching fireside chair at the other side of the hearth.

"First," said Laine, "do you know a Mary Barnes?" He flicked his eyes on the young man's shadowed face.

Turnbull held the book down so that the light caught it. He opened it up, noted the page at which he had been interrupted and deliberately turned to lay the book on the mantel above him.

"I know a young lady by that name."

Barclay leaned forward, his loosely clasped hands tightening between his knees.

"How well?" asked Laine.

"I plan to marry her," said Turnbull, "just as soon as—things are arranged." He pressed the middle finger of his left hand against his left thumb. Then, quickly, he pressed the middle finger of his right hand against his right thumb.

"Oh," said Laine.

"Any more questions?" Turnbull tapped his left foot twice. Then he tapped his right foot twice.

"Yes," said Laine. "When did you last see Miss Barnes?"

Turnbull turned to stare at Laine as if he were a long sought sum of a column of figures. "Is there something the matter with Mary?" he asked sharply. When Laine didn't answer, he clenched one fist, then the other. "I saw her two weeks ago. No. Three weeks ago—now, tell me."

"She's dead." Laine rose slowly and stood next to him. "Someone killed her."

"—that brother—"

Laine sucked in his breath.

"—or her stupid, uneducated uncle." Turnbull rubbed one side of his jaw with his left hand, then he rubbed the other side with his right hand.

Barclay leaned forward, his eyes steady.

"It breaks up the design," said Turnbull with a catch in his voice. "It upsets my calculations and throws the equation into a mathematical absurdity." He bit one side of his lip, then, like a balanced machine, the other side.

Laine's eyes left him to take in the room. It was large and the single slab front door was flanked by two matching divans, each with its step table and twin lamps. A pair of identical bookcases faced each other, one on the left wall, the other against the right. The room had the nicety of a conventional design.

That was it!

Laine peered at Turnbull who was hunching one shoulder and then the other. Here was a man so precise, he matched movements. So mathematical, he based everything on a form of double entry, with constant balance, one side against the other. Laine's lip drooped. He pushed his left hand deep into his pocket, then his right hand. He jerked one out immediately.

"She can't be dead," Turnbull whirled on him. "It's a common name—Mary Barnes."

"She's dead, all right," said Lane. "She had the telephone number of the school on her. That's how we happened to come out here. She call you there?"

Turnbull's mouth tightened. "Yes," he said hesitantly. "Of course she called me. Once. Or twice."

"How about her brother? He call you?"

A spasm twitched Turnbull's left eye. Laine wondered if the right would follow suit. "No," he said. "—maybe so. I had a call last week. By the time I got from my classroom to the office to answer the phone, there was no one there—"

Laine nodded. Rocking on the balls of his feet, he reached for a cigarette. "She was strangled," he said conversationally. He snapped his lighter, watching the other over the small, golden flame. "In a cheap hotel room." He closed up the lighter and gestured around the room with his cigarette. "Nice place you have here. It might have been better if you'd married her and brought her here. The hotel room was a hole." Laine took a long drag of his cigarette. He watched the smoke as it drifted from his nostrils. "There was a radio playing in the room—loud." He followed

Turnbull's eyes as they turned toward the mantel and rested on a small portable radio. "Maybe a radio like that one."

"I didn't do it." Turnbull's soft voice took on the sharp edge of panic. "I swear it. I haven't seen Mary for three weeks. I told her then I wouldn't see her until—"

"Until when?"

"Until—" Turnbull jerked his head defiantly. He pulled the knuckle of one hand, then the knuckle of the other. "Until everything was ready for us to be married. I like things nice and even—all balanced. They weren't—yet."

Laine watched Turnbull desperately try to explain without giving an explanation. "It's like an equation," he floundered. "Y times Z equals X, the unknown quantity."

"And what was the unknown quantity?"

Turnbull was silent.

"Was it something that would make you kill her?"

"Look at me," cried Turnbull, and now his voice was no longer soft. "I don't look like a murderer."

"I've seen a lot of 'em," said Laine. "They never look like murderers. They look like bank clerks, factory workers, cops—mathematics teachers—"

"Her brother's the one that did it. He's crazy."

"Why? Why would he want to kill his sister?"

"He thinks he's God, that's why. He hated her and he hated me."

Judas, Laine's mind remembered. "Why did he hate you?"

Laine watched Turnbull's mouth work.

The teacher took off his glasses and wiped them with a snowy handkerchief. "Or her uncle," he went on, "her illiterate, dried-up uncle who had a sense of duty. I'm sorry I ever mixed into such a family. But since I did, I'm sorriest because I can't finish the equation. Make everything come out even. I feel all lopsided." A tear rolled down his face.

Nausea crowded Laine's throat. He wished to God he could run across someone normal, with nice natural vices like drinking and woman-chasing. Something he could understand without feeling like he had to do a scalping act to see inside some brain and find out why the gears were meshed.

"Who is this uncle?" he asked Turnbull. "What's his name and where does he live?" He jerked his head toward Barclay who drew out a notebook and pencil.

"John Mentor," said Turnbull. "I don't know where he lives and I don't know where the brother lives. When Mary—left, he broke up the home. He's a laborer. A hard-working, honest laborer, with a sense of duty." Thoughtfully, Turnbull scratched his left wrist, then his right. "It was an awful home life for Mary. I felt sorry for her."

"Too bad," said Laine, "you didn't feel sorry soon enough to have kept her from getting that pillowslip around her neck."

"Where were you Monday night?" asked Laine.

"Monday? Why, I was right here at home. My mathematics book had come and I spent the evening working some problems."

"All alone, of course."

Turnbull bridled. "Of course, alone."

"So that no one can verify your alibi."

Turnbull swallowed. "Oh, that. So that was when Mary—died."

Laine watched him without expression.

"I remember now. I was up in the front house for a little while. Talking to my landlord."

"At what time?"

"Why, eight-thirty, I guess. About then. I stayed for a half-hour or so."

Laine shrugged his shoulders. "That the best you can do?"

Turnbull's face turned rosy. His jaw set. "If you want to follow up on it and find out what I talked to him about, you'll discover

I'm an innocent man." Folding his arms, Turnbull stared resolutely at the door.

Laine turned to Barclay. "All signs point to the fact that he's clammed up. The next question we ask him, he'll probably answer that he'll have to see his attorney first. Let's get with it."

Barclay heaved himself from the chair. Laine tapped Turnbull's arm. "Don't leave town. Don't even think about it. You'll be watched. If you have anything you want to tell us, call us up. We'll listen. You're probably holding back plenty, but if I know my characters and I think I do, you'll be anxious to spill in about twenty-four hours. Even things up, you know?" Laine placed his card on the coffee table. He looked at Barclay and jerked his head toward the door. They went out together.

"A cluck," pronounced Barclay.

"A prudish stinker with a literal mind," amended Laine. "I don't like prudish stinkers with literal minds—I don't like Turnbull."

They went through the gate and along the hedge. "Just a minute," said Laine. He turned off on the flagged walk which led to the big house and pushed the buzzer. The door opened.

"Didn't you find him?" asked the flat voice. "I thought sure he was there."

"We found him," said Laine. "He said you could alibi him for last Monday night. Can you?"

The man's arm reached back around the door and switched on the outside light. He scrutinized Laine with eyes the color of sloe gin.

"I'm with the Sheriff's Office," explained Laine. "Now— about Monday—"

"Oh, yes." Laine could smell the man's pre-dinner cocktail. "Monday—Mr. Turnbull was in to see me that night—about nine, I think. I'm sorry to lose him—"

"Are you going to?"

"Well, as soon as he gets married, he'll have to vacate. That's what we were talking about. He wants to bring his wife here—and I was reluctant. A bachelor's no trouble, but—" The man spread his hands which had a slight tremble. "A wife's something else again. Then, when he said there was a child—" The man shook his head. "I don't want any kids around. I guess the woman he's marrying has one by a previous marriage."

"Or maybe," said Laine, "she had one without a marriage."

The man's laugh was as acrid as a mixture of scotch and gin-gerale. "That I'm not interested in," he said definitely, "how she got her kid makes no difference. I just don't want it here."

"Well," said Laine, "did Turnbull see your point of view?"

"I'm afraid not. He was quite bitter." The man's voice ran on like a rivulet of beer over an uneven table. "He likes the place back there. He says it has a good, geometrical design. It is nice, too, and I want to keep it that way. I don't want any brat's teeth marks in the woodwork and I don't want the flowers torn up. Turnbull was a good tenant. Took care of things. He doesn't want to give it up. Says he likes it because the doors center the walls and the windows make a design—he acted like it was a case of the woman and child against the house and when he left that night, it looked to me like the house was winning." Again, he spread his shaking hands. "I don't much care. I can get me another bachelor back there. I did like Turnbull, though. A mathematician never gets into trouble."

"Don't kid yourself," said Laine as he backed off the front steps.

"Come on," he said to Barclay. Out at the curbing, he hesi-tated. "Maybe he killed her so he wouldn't have to marry her. Maybe we'd better haul him in." Then he opened the car door. "No," he decided.

When they were halfway across the pass, Barclay said, out of his long silence, "What was that gibberish about Y and Z and X?" he asked.

The car swerved under Laine's hands. A warning horn sounded.

"X," said Laine, speeding up, "X is the child I'll bet my right leg. X is the little girl, the unknown quantity…"

CHAPTER SEVENTEEN

I t was a murky Sunday morning. Laine again watched the licking flames of the fireplace behind the golden-linked screen. He watched the flames so that he wouldn't watch the red hair which pushed its color through the corner of his eyes. The flames were the only light in the room and the shadows were trying to lull Laine's suspicions.

"I can't imagine, Mr. Laine," said the woman, "why you feel you have to question me again about the prowler. I don't know the man. I can only suppose he was planning a burglary."

Laine's face was busy with his thoughts.

She laughed lightly and the sound was a tinkle. "There have been prowlers before in this neighborhood and there will be prowlers again. Why should this one be so important?"

That decided him. He turned in his chair and faced the woman. The flames had built a nimbus about her hair, burning it to copper and golden light. They leaped against her creamy skin, to widen her eyes.

Laine cleared his throat. "He's important, Mrs. Thurmond," he began formally, "because he may be a cog in the wheel."

She moved closer and Laine moved back. "You may be another."

Laine suddenly became angry with this woman whose beauty bothered him. "There was a girl," he said, biting his words savagely, "who was killed in a crummy hotel because a bunch of people had made a sucker out of her."

Now his listener sat tense before him. He wondered if she had read the item about Mary Barnes in the newspaper. Or had she killed the girl herself? He wondered if Mockley had told her because he had read the item. Or had he killed the girl himself?

Laine wanted to hurt Mrs. Thurmond, to crush all her beauty, to bequeath her with appalling ugliness. "The first one to make a sucker out of her was a guy she must have loved. He left her to have her baby alone." Laine gestured apathetically. "He started things. Then she had to have a place to have her baby. And a doctor reached out a helping hand..."

Mrs. Thurmond's face was a mask in the firelight.

"Now this doctor," he went on in his story-telling voice, "had a neat little set-up. He sold the babies of unfortunate mothers to motherless women who were more fortunate. This particular baby was destined for a woman who needed it to gain an inheritance." Laine leaned forward to stare at Mrs. Thurmond. She was so still he couldn't see her breathe. Only her eyes were alive.

"Now the woman who wanted the inheritance wanted it so badly that she was not only willing to barter in human lives, but she tempted a doctor of her acquaintance to be an accessory after the fact by bribing him at a time when he was weak with the weakness of facing financial ruin."

Laine settled again. God, the woman was beautiful!

"Did you kill her, Mrs. Thurmond? Did you kill her because she came to you, pleading for her child? Did you wrap that pillowcase around her throat because she threatened to expose you and knock down your shining piles of money right in the lap of your husband's stepbrother? Did you carve the bloody mark upon her bosom for her temerity in daring to threaten your security?"

Mrs. Thurmond's suddenly expelled breath was a small explosion. "No." Her head jerked as if he had struck her.

He bent over, staring her in the eyes, his elbows on his knees. "Where were you last Monday night?"

"I? Why, I don't know."

"You'd better remember, and see that other people remember it too. You need an alibi."

"Why, I was downtown shopping. The stores—they stay open 'til nine now. Yes, I was downtown Christmas shopping."

"The stores stay open 'til nine, yes. Then where were you? Where were you until midnight?"

Mrs. Thurmond sat still. She opened her mouth and closed it again.

"Call your maid," snapped Laine. "Call the maid who would have been up to let you in."

She didn't move.

"Call her," repeated Laine, "or I'll go through this house and get them all together."

Mrs. Thurmond rose and walked automatically to the archway of the room, Laine behind her. A maid materialized as if a lamp had been rubbed. Her eyes were frightened, watching Laine, who stepped in front of her mistress. He blotted out any gestures of warning as he stood before the girl.

"Where was Mrs. Thurmond last Monday night?" he asked.

The maid's eyes clouded as she tried to see around his body.

"Answer him, Loretta." From his shoulder, Mrs. Thurmond's voice was weary.

"Why, I don't remember."

"You will," suggested Laine. "Just think. You will."

The maid was quiet. "Let's see," she murmured. Then she looked up brightly. "Oh, yes. That's the night you brought the baby her little blue radio—"

Laine opened his mouth and took in some nice, fresh air.

"Yes." The maid looked directly at Laine. "Mrs. Thurmond went shopping."

"What time?"

"Directly after an early dinner. About seven-thirty. She took the convertible and drove alone."

"And she bought a radio."

"Yes, sir. It was a surprise."

"Yes," said Laine thoughtfully, "you can say that again. What time did she get home?"

"I dropped off to sleep. She let herself in."

He turned. "What time did you get home?"

"About 11:30."

"Where were you?"

"Driving around."

"Just driving around. No witnesses to that?"

"None."

"I'll be damned." Laine looked at her. She was still a beautiful woman but a scared beautiful woman.

CHAPTER EIGHTEEN

Laine walked over the grounds and through the gate. He saw the official cars at their posts. The fog had turned to mist as he turned into the neighboring driveway and up the flagstoned path. The office end of the residence had a small light burning in the morning gloom. Laine followed the path to the main entrance of the house. He rang the bell.

"I want to see Dr. Mockley," he told the butler.

"I'm sorry, sir." The butler looked him over with quick eyes and discarded what they saw. "Dr. Mockley is resting. If it's a professional call, his office hours are…"

Laine pushed the man aside. "It is a professional call," he snarled, "but it happens to be my profession. Tell Dr. Mockley Inspector Laine of the Sheriff's Office wants to see him on professional business." Laine snapped his fingers under the butler's flaring nostrils. He waited in the entrance hall, gazing about at what decent money could buy and indecent money could keep. Dr. Mockley walked in.

"I want to talk with you," said Laine.

"So I gathered. What about?"

"I'll be damned if I'm going to stand here and tell you. Somewhere we can sit down. It might take awhile." Laine's skin crawled. His fingers itched. He followed Mockley into a drawing room, waiting until the doctor seated himself before he took a chair to face him.

"You sold a baby to Mrs. Thurmond in July of 1951," he said abruptly.

"That's absurd." The doctor started to rise.

"Sit down," barked Laine.

The doctor sat.

"You sold her Mary Barnes' baby so she could latch onto the inheritance Scotty Thurmond left. You contacted Dr. Ten Eyck and he got the baby for you."

"Oh, come now. I'm an ethical doctor. What is this, blackmail?"

"Mrs. Thurmond got the inheritance. You got enough money from her to pay a lawsuit which was threatening your security and Ten Eyck got a nice piece of change—Mary Barnes got death."

Dr. Mockley was staring at him. "You must be crazy."

Laine waited, his fingers writhing.

"And you can't prove it."

"The hell I can't and the hell I'm not going to. I'm going to smash you, Mockley. I'm going to smash everybody who's touched his dirty fingers in this business. I've handled all kinds. I've handled highjackers, thieves and killers. I always said the rapists were the scummiest of the lot. Well, now I put the baby racketeers next in line. I don't like 'em." Laine growled. "I don't like you."

"Now, listen here … Let's see your warrant."

Laine was mad. Laine was furious. He reached over and slapped the doctor's face. The sound was a staccato exclamation point to his feelings, the print of his hand a rosy punctuation mark on a white cheekbone.

CHAPTER NINETEEN

Sunday papers strewed the apartment. Laine sat in the midst of them. Barclay across the room. Barclay's face was wine-colored from the outdoor air. "Awful cold for California," he observed. "Awful cold."

Laine reached over to turn on a reading lamp. It was not yet dark outside, but the room drifted with the shadow of oncoming twilight.

"So you let Barnes go," said Laine.

"Yeah. No legitimate answers to our calls." He shook his head. "Too bad. We've hit a few snags."

"Got a good man trailing him?"

"Oh, sure. I don't think there'll be any hitches. You never can tell, though."

"No. You never can tell."

"So Mockley didn't raise a holler."

"No." Laine grinned wrily. "I must have been nuts to hit the guy that way. God, he could have made it tough for me."

"Prob'ly scared to."

"Sure. He's got qualms. I'd like to know where he was last Monday night. I'd like to know if he was up there in that hotel."

"You and me both."

"How long ago did you release Barnes?"

"Just before I came up here."

"How'd he act?"

"As usual. Nuts."

"Maybe he won't even go home. Maybe he'll hole up some-where and we won't find out anything."

"Oh, he'll prob'ly lead us—" Barclay's mouth stayed open as he listened to a shrill scream from the street.

Laine sat tense. They heard the mumbling and muttering of a gathering crowd below through closed windows.

"What in hell's going on out there?" cried Laine. He was across the room and down the stairs, Barclay ponderously pur-suing him.

The street was now dusky with evening—the time of day when vision is distorted between the light and the dark. A small group of people had collected on the sidewalk about twenty feet away. As Laine galloped toward it, he wondered how they could gather so quickly in this quiet district. He pushed through and stopped.

Lying there on the cold concrete, he saw first the spraying flame of hair, then Mrs. Thurmond's sprawled legs, like those of a rag doll thrown aside by a forgetful child.

"Okay now. Get back," he snapped at the onlookers. He saw their bulging eyes—their craned necks.

"Get back, you," he yelled as he pushed at the audience.

"Here. Who you shovin'?"

"I'm shovin you. Now, scram." Laine saw Barclay on the edge. "Barclay," he called, "it's the Thurmond dame. Hop down to that drug store and get the ambulance."

"Hurt bad?" grunted Barclay as he started to jog down the street.

"Don't know. She's cut."

"Now, get back," he again told the crowd. "Let the lady have some air."

"Who're you?" Again that pugnacious tone.

"Listen, bud." Laine's voice shook. "I'm a special investigator. Want to make something of it?"

He knelt down beside the tangled red hair. He saw a pulsating movement of the creamy throat just above the silver fur. It moved jouncingly—fast, then slow as if it couldn't quite make up its mind. He could see her cloudy breath, like ectoplasm from ghost pale lips. He shivered. He had forgotten to be cold.

Barclay returned and was pushing the crowd aside with his bulk. The people moved backward, whispering among themselves.

"How bad is she?" asked Barclay as he leaned over.

"Not sure. See the blood?" A thin scarlet line had separated itself from the blazing hair. It coursed waveringly and found a crack in the sidewalk down which to run.

Laine stood up and faced the group of people. They were now lined up before the stucco front of an apartment house, wide-eyed, the half-smiles showing their interest at this drama of a dull Sunday.

"Anybody hear anything? Or see anything?" asked Laine.

"I did." A youth stepped forward. His pimples stood out at this bit of limelight thrown upon him. "I was coming out of there." He pointed to the hallway in the apartment building. "I saw the woman fall and I thought I saw someone run to one of the cars. Then the car started up and went down the street." The boy looked toward the curbing. "That's where the car was. Double-parked next to that green convertible."

Laine turned. He walked to the convertible, leaned over the steering wheel and struck a match. When the flame flickered out, he moved slowly over toward Barclay. He looked down at the girl. "It's her car," he said softly.

"Could you describe whoever it was that drove away?" he asked the witness.

The boy's face lengthened. Now his expression was hardly discernible in the shadows. "No, I can't. I didn't even see him hit her. I just figured he must have when I saw her fall and he ran away."

"You're sure it was a 'he'?"

"Oh, yeah." The boy hesitated. "I don't know how I know. Maybe by the way he ran. A man runs different than a woman. But it was a man, all right."

"Take his name and address, Barclay," said Laine. Barclay moved toward the boy. Laine addressed the onlookers. "Anybody else see anything?"

"Guess not," came a man's voice. "We all came out of apartments around here. Heard the scream and came running. But we didn't see anything. Only her lying there."

The shrill scream of a siren cut through the night. The people backed closer to the building. Barclay and Laine stood over the victim. The ambulance slithered to a stop.

Two men stepped to the sidewalk. One of them trained a flashlight on the figure. He raised the beam to take in Laine and Barclay. "Oh, it's you," he said. "What goes on here?"

"We don't know," said Barclay, "I'll be down to the receiving hospital in a little while and give you the dope."

The white coated attendant stooped.

"What do you think?" asked Laine.

"Can't tell. You don't know what happened?"

"Well, we figure she was hit over the head."

"Mm-hm. Might be a fracture. Might be a concussion. Could be just an abrasion and she's in shock. We'll take her along. You can come down later. By then, we can probably tell you something."

"Okay," said Laine. He moved away. "You can go home now," he told the line of watchers. "Show's over."

"Come on, Barclay. You left your coat in my apartment."

They walked back silently. Laine turned the heater up in the paper strewn room. Barclay shivered. "Gettin' colder," he said.

"Damn cold." Laine looked at Barclay. "What do you make of that down there? Do you think she was on her way to see me?"

"Looks like it, unless she's got some other business around here. I think, though, she came to tell you something..."

"Or make a deal," said Laine.

"Yeah." Barclay folded his coat, laying it on the arm of the chair, and settled. "Maybe she did want to make a deal. She was pretty and you're a sucker."

Laine half-rose. "Do you think...?" he began.

Barclay waved him down. "No. I don't think you'd deal. I just think she knew you were female-conscious. She hoped you'd deal. I'm sorry she didn't make it."

The phone rang. Laine grabbed it. "Yes," he said, the instrument halfway to his face.

"Barclay? He's here. Just a minute."

"It's Gleason," he said as he handed the phone over. "He sounds worried."

"Gleason," answered Barclay into the mouthpiece. "What in hell happened out there? How'd you let the Thurmond dame get away?" He listened, the knuckles of his hand growing white as he clenched the phone. "Sure we know about it. She was conked on the dome right out here in front of Laine's apartment."

Laine saw Barclay's face sag without losing its impassivity. "The hell you say," he said softly. "Well, I'll be damned. You guys are better at chasin' marbles... hell no, the damage is done now. Go back on the job. Sure, I know you've got a couple of empty houses to watch. But watch 'em and grab Mockley when he gets back—if he gets back—and give him a quick goin' over. Give it to him fast before he's got time to catch his breath. Scare the pants off him." He slammed the phone down.

"So Mockley's gone, too." Laine's voice was expressionless.

"Yeah. Seems Thurmond came out of her driveway hellbent for election. It upset the boys, so they both followed her. When one of the cars came to and found they were makin' a parade of things, it came back to discover the Mockley car gone from the garage..."

"Then?"

"Then the car that tailed the convertible, lost it."

"How could they do it?" Laine said. "The car was like a target. Like a green 'go' sign."

Barclay laughed shortly. "The driver used to be on the traffic squad. Maybe he saw a speeder—threw him off gear."

"So Mockley's out and Mrs. Thurmond gets knocked cold. That ties the picture together."

"Well." Barclay sighed and hunched himself to his feet. He picked up the coat and slung it over his shoulder. "Might as well get down to the Receiving Hospital and see how she is."

Laine was thinking. He looked up suddenly. "Wonder if everything's smooth with Barnes' tail?"

Barclay stared down glassily. "You think of pleasant things."

"Why don't you phone down and see?"

Barclay dropped his coat to the chair again and slouched over to the phone. He picked it up and dialed the number. "Things don't happen that way," he told Laine. "The whole bottom don't drop out at once. It goes in little pieces... Oh, this is Barclay. Any report come in yet about Barnes?... Huh?" He drew his lower lip over his upper, sucking thoughtfully. "Yeah. I see..." He looked down at his shoes, shining the toe of one against his trouser leg. "Okay. That's that." Laying the phone back gently, he turned carefully to let himself down in the chair, as if he were afraid of breaking a bone.

Barclay looked up. Although his face was still expressionless, his eyes were bewildered. "Lost him, too. Seems Barnes went into some Mission downtown and God only knows how he got out again or where he went, but the tail is still goin' around in circles."

"Now we've got two men who could have wanted Mrs. Thurmond out of the way." Laine reached for a cigarette. His hand stopped midway. "Two?" he asked himself softly. "I wonder where Dr. Ten Eyck is now?"

Barclay groaned. He stood up. "You worry about him. He's your property. I'm goin' to visit the Receiving Hospital."

CHAPTER TWENTY

By the light of the moon, Laine rolled along the crest of the arroyo, remembering this journey through drenching storm. The evening's events kept walking through his mind, walking through and dancing jigs. He reached the top of the canyon. The countryside cascaded up one side and poured down the other, shimmering in the moonlight.

The road was almost empty with so few headlights peeking over the rim to come rushing toward him, that those few were startling. He found his nerves slithering and discovered himself weary.

At last he reached the asphalt road which led to the lonely Ten Eyck house.

A car, lightless, parked on the shoulder, stopped him.

"Gus?" he called.

"Gus is parked on the other side. That you, Mr. Laine?"

"Oh, Drake. Yes, it's me." Laine stepped from his car to meet the other in the center of the moonlit road.

"All quiet up there at the house?"

"As a mouse."

"You sure Ten Eyck hasn't slipped out and vanished somewhere?"

"Not unless he went down some other road and there's no other road. What's the matter? You jittery?"

"Damn right," said Laine. "Everything's as mixed up in town as a bride's reactions. Headquarters sends out all its nearsighted men to tail our suspects—or maybe they just wear dark glasses like the movie stars ..."

"You mean they lost someone?"

"Three of 'em. I just wondered if Ten Eyck had given you the slip and we could claim a hundred percent."

Laine stepped into his car. "Think I'll go up there and talk to him. You might follow me and stand by outside. I don't expect any trouble, though." Laine started his motor. The other car's lights beamed down the side of the road. Driving toward the gate, with the headlights following him, Laine turned in and parked.

He pushed the buzzer and while he re-read the nameplate, he listened to the soft, echoing chimes. The door opened and Laine stepped in closing it behind him.

The maid looked as young and clean as a sapling in the sunshine. She was as fragrant as new leaves. She stepped back, startled.

"I want to talk to Dr. Ten Eyck."

"And who shall I say ..."

"Just go get him. I'm waiting."

Laine meandered through the hall and into a large living room. His eyes took in the books on the shelves—rapidly, but thoroughly. He moved around, scanning the tables and a desk, riffling through sheet music on the spinet in the corner.

"Looking for something?" The voice was starched silk.

Laine turned slowly to again rock back with the symmetry of a face centered by a dark widow's peak.

"Just amusing myself." Laine walked over to settle in the corner of a divan. "Sit down," he invited his host. "We have something to discuss."

"I don't know that we have." Ten Eyck sat stiffly on a chair by a reading table, drumming the shining top with gleaming fingernails. "I don't know that we have anything to discuss."

"Well, you gave me kind of rough treatment the last time I was here. We could discuss that."

"I don't know what you mean." Ten Eyck's eyes turned blank. "You were a stranger. You came to my laboratory ... talking incoherently. When I discovered your condition, however, I forgave that. How are you now?"

"I'm fine," said Laine brightly. "My feelings are hurt, though. I'm sensitive about being bashed on the head."

"Surely you're joking." The doctor raised his perfect brows to his perfect hairline. "You were a sick man when you entered my laboratory. Quite delirious." Ten Eyck smiled faintly in Laine's direction. "It was a stormy night." He shook his head. "No night for a man with a rising temperature to be out in the rain."

Laine sat quietly, watching and waiting. "My temperature was rising, all right," he agreed. "It's rising again."

"I'm surprised to see you on your feet," continued the doctor. "You were on the verge of pneumonia ... fever ... delirium ..."

"So that's the way it is," said Laine. "I'm a walking virus. I picked up a scrap of paper that had Mary Barnes' name on it—from a gutter, maybe? Huh-uh. It was a page from your book of patients."

Ten Eyck looked kindly at him. "I have no book of patients," he smiled. "I am a retired physician. The hospital I own is a laboratory—a playroom of sorts. A hobby."

"Oh, sure."

"I don't know what you think you remember," the doctor bent close in confidence. "But you were a very sick man that night. You passed out. I left the room to get help so that I could put you to bed and when I returned, you were gone. I've been worried about you, out in that rain and driving a car—"

"I'll bet, with me delirious that way."

The doctor smiled. "Can you prove otherwise?"

Laine's thoughts skittered. "I'm surprised to find you home, Ten Eyck."

"Where else should I be? The cars you've stationed on the road keep me hemmed in."

"So you know about them?"

"It wasn't difficult." The doctor examined his glowing finger-nails. "My wife was followed when she went into town."

"She noticed?"

"It was obvious enough."

"Only if she expected to be followed. Only if she knew your business was such that she might be."

The doctor shined his nails to brighter luster against an immaculate coat lapel.

"But, Dr. Ten Eyck," Laine leaned back negligently, his eyes sharp, "the baby racket which you're trying to tell me is so effectively zero now is only a small part of my investigation." He sat straight, stiffening his body to match the concentration of his eyes. "I happen to be checking up on a matter of murder."

Laine could see no small flicker of either surprise or fear. "Mary Barnes' murder." Then it came, the light in the eyes like a funeral pyre. "She was the girl who came to you a few days ago to ask for information about her baby. You didn't give it to her. But Carlotta Conti did."

Ten Eyck's face was blank.

"We found Mary Barnes' body in a Los Angeles hotel. There was a bloody X on her breast. Your signature?"

"No." The doctor's face squirmed with what he had heard. "It's not true."

"What's not true? She's dead. She's in the morgue now." Laine stood and bent over the crouched figure. "Where were you Monday night?"

"I was right here." The doctor's words tapped like the hammer of a cap gun against its own sides. "Right here. I had a patient…"

"No, you didn't," Laine grinned. "You're retired, remember? Your hospital is a hobby room."

The doctor's mouth opened and jerked. "My wife was sick. I was with her. I was right here at home."

"Get your witnesses." Laine folded his arms to wait. The doctor tried to rise and failed.

"Okay." Laine walked to the hallway, his eyes upon the man in the chair.

"Mrs. Ten Eyck," he bawled down the corridor.

Looks like *The Thinker,* thought Laine, glancing back at the man sagged in his chair, except this one's trying not to think. He walked to the stairway and looked up. Its spiral wound to the upper floor, supported only by its own construction. "Mrs. Ten Eyck," he called upward, wondering if his voice would negotiate the turns.

At last she appeared, standing straight and still, her hand on the lacy bannister above. Her ash blonde hair was not by contrast, but a continuation of pale and disrupted madonna features. The face was drained of expression, not as if it had been but recently washed of life, but as if, little by little, the capacity of both joy and sorrow had been rinsed from it.

Laine lowered his voice adding to it the hushed quality reserved for the dying. "Would you come down here, please, Mrs. Ten Eyck?"

She came, the soft gray draperies of her gown a lazy cloud spray about her slim body. Laine wanted to get away from her. He felt the sudden need of healthy emotion.

He walked into the living room, and the sight of the doctor gave him his anger. The woman stood close, yet apart from her husband. Laine looked at the man, to ball his fists. He looked at the woman, to feel his flesh crawl up his spine and raise the hairs on the back of his neck.

"Just one question," he said harshly, wanting to shake her into listening. "Just one. Think before you answer and answer truthfully." Laine waited as he would with a small child, to let understanding sift through. "Where was your husband on last Monday night?"

"At home," she said immediately, her eyes pale wells of emptiness.

"He said you were sick."

"I suppose so," she said listlessly. "I am sick. All the time."

"I'll check that." Laine backed toward the doorway. "I'll check it with your servants. I have a man on your front terrace. Don't try to go anywhere."

As he walked down the hallway, he brushed his clothes with quick, impatient flicks of his fingers, and rubbed his palms together in a scrubbing motion. He inhaled deeply, then expelled his breath in a cool puff of wind before his face. The house was very quiet.

He pushed open a swinging door upon the bright tiles of a kitchen. Standing at the sink, her arms flecked with soapsuds, stood the little maid who had admitted him. She looked up, startled.

A nice, healthy task, thought Laine, washing dishes—and a vivid, alive girl to do it.

"Hello," he said.

She picked up a cloth and dried her arms, staring at him.

"Swell couple you work for. I don't know how you keep your sanity."

Her brows drew together and her eyes searched him. She placed the cloth on the tiled counter and backed up against the sink.

"Dr. Ten Eyck," Laine told her, "is suspected on a murder charge."

The girl placed the back of her still damp hand to her lips, her eyes wide over it.

"So I want to know where he was last Monday night. Where was he?"

"Why—why..."

Laine could see her searching back through the days. Mentally, as she studied, he counted back—Saturday, Friday, Thursday, Wednesday, Tuesday, Monday...

"He was here," said the girl, lowering her hand. "Right here."

"You sure?" But he knew she was, he'd seen her mind back up. Laine dropped his shoulders and unclenched his hands. He looked at them, surprised. Then he straightened, all of him, listening. Quickly he stepped to the swinging door and gave it a push. He heard rising voices—not the words—tumbling, battling, rushing like tide water—the one pitched high and the other a placating rumble. Laine strode down the corridor and stopped as the words became clear.

Leaning against the wall, he concentrated on the words that bounced from the living room entrance, beat against the walls of the hall and held him rigid. He could not see the speakers, but he could hear. And he could feel the little maid as she moved close to him, the brush of her arm on his hand.

"... you rotten devil," came the evenly spaced words, followed by an undercurrent of protestation. "You rotten devil," came the repeated sound. Then suddenly, high pitched, "You rotten, black-hearted, cold-blooded, venom-pocked devil..." Laine pushed forward, hearing the dual words like double steps on a stairway of unreason.

"I set you up in business. Remember that? My money set you up ..." Laine rocked back and waited. "... set you up in a decent profession. My money. But you weren't satisfied. Not you. Not to be decent. You had to make it nasty and rotten. You took my money and made it rotten. Made me rotten, too. Alone and lonely ..."

"Griselda!" The man's voice pushed through at last. "I did it for you. I wanted to give it back. Griselda! No!"

"You've turned all the love I had for you ..." and the words were lost in a sudden stunning roar.

Laine placed the palms of his hands against the wall and catapulted forward. The front door flew open. Drake yelled. Running, Laine reached the opening into the living room.

The woman stood in there, the hem of her cloud-gray draperies wet with blood as they rested upon the figure at her feet.

She turned her face toward Laine, its stillness now broken. Now it was alive—eyes blazing—cheeks flushed. She raised the gun to her ash-blonde hair...

Laine staggered into the room, through trails of misty smoke. He looked down into a face which was now featureless, a red marshland with its worms of torn flesh. He looked down at the revolver on the carpet, a tiny toy with a pearl handle, light enough to conceal in the draperies of a gown. Deadly enough to kill.

Laine's groping hand found himself a chair apart from the two. He saw the maid, wide-eyed, at the doorway. "Get out, you little fool," he yelled. He looked at Drake. Drake's face held a tinge of bilious color, but he was on his feet.

"I can't stand it," groaned Laine. "Drake, check Ten Eyck. See if he's gone. I know she is." Without wanting to, he could see Drake stoop, his fumbling hands, his fingers on a limp wrist—his shaking head.

"Hell, he's dead. It went right through the heart."

"What heart?" asked Laine.

CHAPTER TWENTY-ONE

L aine sat watching the little maid. All, now, that remained of her tears were the streaked cheeks, the swollen eyes. Her sobs had become nervous hiccoughs, growing farther apart and less violent. The sounds from the living room were quiet ones, a subdued cleaning up of hysteria. The men in there moved softly as they took their pictures and searched with authoritative fingers.

"Now...feeling a little better?" Laine thought he should ask himself that question. A milkman's job might be a pleasant, uninteresting routine if only you didn't have to get up so early.

The girl nodded.

"Pretty tough, seeing that," sympathized Laine. "I'm sorry you had to." He rubbed the palms of his hands. "You're sure of what you told me before—aren't you? That Dr. Ten Eyck was here all day Monday and Monday night?"

"Yes, sir." Laine noticed that her emotional upset had not interfered with her prettiness.

"Where are the rest of them?" he asked, "Surely there is a staff of servants in a place like this. Where are they? There's been enough noise to wake the dead." He clamped down his lips, cutting off the last word sharply.

"There were two others. The cook and another maid. Dr. Ten Eyck laid them off." It was—let me see—it was Tuesday night. Yes, the night it rained so hard. Wasn't that Tuesday?"

Laine nodded.

The girl's clasped hands in her lap folded and unfolded. "I thought it was kind of funny, the way he made them go so suddenly—out in the rain and all. He hurried them..."

"He had to," said Laine. He was remembering that rainy night, and how busy Ten Eyck must have been after his departure. "They probably knew too much."

"About what?"

Laine smiled. "How long have you been here?"

"Oh, not long," she said, "only about a month."

"They'd been here a long time, though, hadn't they?"

"I guess thay had. Sometimes they'd go over to the hospital to help clean. I wasn't supposed to, though. I've never been in the hospital."

Laine leaned over to tap her knee. "That's why you weren't kicked out in the rain, too, Baby." He stood up. "I think you'd better pack your things. You don't want to stay here any longer."

She shuddered.

"I'll have one of the men take you wherever you want to go. Now you just holler when you're ready." He started out the door, then he looked back at her, small and forlorn in the big chair. "You'd better get yourself a job with a nice mediocre family, a family that lives happily and is happy living."

He looked through and into the living room. A sheet shrouded the mounded center of the rug. A lamp had been overturned and a long scarlet streak confused the pattern of its shade.

"Gus."

"Yes, Mr. Laine."

"I told that little girl to pack up her duds. You take her where she wants to go when she's ready."

"Will do, Mr. Laine."

"And, listen," Laine took a step into the room. "I don't know how she's fixed for dough. She may be on the spot. Give her this if she needs it." Laine handed out a folded bill.

"Drake," Laine called as he stepped back into the hallway. Drake joined him.

"I want you to go over to the hospital with me. That place needs a little attention."

CHAPTER TWENTY-TWO

"Wonder why she did it?" pondered Drake as Laine pulled out of the driveway.

"Mrs. Ten Eyck?" Laine was silent a long time. "You know those firecrackers you used to light when you were a boy? You'd throw them, then they'd sizzle and seem to go out? And just when you figured them for a dud and walked over to pick one up, it'd explode in your face …?"

Drake looked at Laine curiously. "What's that got to do with Mrs. Ten Eyck?"

"She was the dud that went off."

Drake shook his head in the darkness of the car.

"She was probably nuts about her husband. From what I could gather when she was going through her Ophelia scene, she'd turned over her money to him to establish a practice—then when he went into his baby racket, she figured he'd dirtied up her money—and her, too."

"Yeah, but what's that got to do with firecrackers?"

"Hell, you're as bad as Barclay. "Well," he said patiently, "She was sort of an idealist, at least she had her ethics, and probably she'd raised this Ten Eyck up to some kind of a pedestal …"

"Her idol," supplied Drake. "Yes. A tin god. Then he up and blasted all her conceptions."

"So she blasted him?"

Laine shuddered and twisted the car toward the grove of trees.

"Well, before that, she'd turned escapist—she kind of drew a protective shell around her. She blunted all her sensations so she couldn't feel any more." Laine was conscious of his companion's non-understanding. He stopped the car and turned off the motor, to finish lamely, "then the shell just broke and the dud went off." Laine stepped onto the now hard-packed road. The moon had traveled over the arch of the sky and was framed by clouds." The building, outlined with silver on its rise of ground, peeked forth from one shining eye.

"Guess somebody's there," said Laine. He walked onto the porch and tried the door. It opened at his touch. He fumbled about the wall for the light switch and pressed his lips tight as he looked around the bright and familiar room.

"This is where the doctor put me to sleep," he told Drake. Drake held his gun, gum-shoeing his way toward the dark opening.

"Not taking any chances, are you?" observed Laine.

Drake clicked on a flash, circling each room with its spot of amber as they entered. They flooded the cubicles with light on passing through. The iron beds were dismantled, the mattresses rolled tidily to stand upright on each set of springs. Laine shook his head wonderingly. "Ten Eyck and his crew were busy Tuesday night."

"The hospital was dark when we got here," said Drake. "You told me to check. We did."

"Yes. They worked fast. Had to trundle a few patients out of here, too—maybe some babies and get rid of a couple of servants. Probably a nurse or two."

"Jeez. You think he killed 'em?"

Laine laughed. "No. I just think he paid them off. God knows what he did with the maternity cases. We haven't had any reports of pregnant women lying in the ditch?"

This, Drake seriously considered. "No," he decided, "we haven't."

"He probably had a contact. Some other nursing home. Or some other get-rich-quick quack." Laine looked down at a cot with chromium handholds. They appeared to be stirrups on tight springs.

"This is the labor room," said Drake.

Laine looked at the stirrups again. "Gee," he said.

"And here's the nursery."

Laine took in the row of baskets on standards. They looked like small clothes baskets to him. Blankets were piled in a corner by the scales. A box with a glass window stood nearby.

"An incubator," informed Drake.

Well, I thought they used incubators for chickens."

"And premature babies."

Laine looked at his companion. "How come you know so much about this business?"

"I've been a father six times."

As a shuffling noise whispered in from the hallway, both men whirled, facing the door, guns ready in their hands, faces ready for anything.

Into the opening dragged a grotesquerie whose cheekbones looked as if they would push through the yellow flesh, whose hospital gown was smudged and torn at the neck as if soiled fingers had been clutching and pulling at it for a long time as they were doing now, whose feet faltered in an agony of effort on legs which were trembling bare stems beneath the revealing brevity of the gown. He came toward them in a slow and painful shamble.

"My God, what's that?" asked Drake.

"That's Pop. He needs a shot."

"He needs something." Drake kept his finger on the trigger.

"Gotta have a pinch o' powder," whined Pop. "If I don't—I'll tear the place wide open," and he lunged weakly, his eyes, trying to focus, rolled with the effort.

"What's the matter with the doc? Didn't he take care of you?"

"He ain't been near me all day." Pop sank to his bony knees in a torment.

"Pretty bad, aren't you?" observed Laine as he looked down at the violent agitations of the man's body.

Pop placed his hands on the floor and crept toward Laine's feet, a maudlin maze of a crawl. "You can beat me if you'll jus' give me a sniff... jus' one little one... I'll let you stomp me in the ground... for jus' one little one..."

Laine swallowed, his face rippling with disgust. Drake had stepped back and out of the way.

"We'll take you to a doctor," said Laine, not looking down. "He'll help you out."

Pop laid his cheek on the linoleum floor, his breath sobbing between his lips. "Gotta have it now. Can't wait... Doc's got some. Safe... it's locked."

Laine's eyes turned business-like. "Safe," he said to Drake. "Think you can open it?"

Drake's lips rolled. "What're you gonna do? Fix this guy up? You can't."

"I don't care about him," Laine said, jerking his head toward the groveling man. "I want to know where the safe is, and I want to get into it."

"Well, if it can be opened, I can do it. Some of 'em are crack-proof, you know. It might need dynamite."

"On your feet, Pop." Laine grabbed hold of the shoulder of the slack hospital gown. "Take his other arm, Drake. He's limp as a wilted rhubarb."

Drake pocketed his gun to move slowly toward the half-suspended figure. "Don't like to touch him." They trundled their burden from the room.

"Tell us where to, Pop," said Laine. "Tell us where the safe is."

"Safe... Gonna get it... gonna get it... in the deliv... the deliv..."

"The delivery room," interpreted Drake. "That lighted one, maybe?"

They stopped at the doorway. The bed had been made up with sheets and blankets. Now it looked like someone had had a Dali dream on it. Clothes were scattered about the floor. A water glass had been broken, its slivers shining like tears.

"Pop's room," said Laine. "Must be the other. It's the only one we haven't seen."

They turned on the light and looked about, the rumpled figure a dead weight between them.

"Don't look like there's any safe in here," said Drake as he gazed about the room. The light over the delivery table was dazzling and brought answering gleams from the instruments and the weird tools of birth.

Laine shook the handicap between them. "Wake up, Pop," he commanded. "Make like you're alive. Where's the safe?"

The bleary eyes slitted open. "Safe... safe..." He jerked from their arms and staggered toward a sterilizing cabinet.

"Superhuman strength," commented Laine. "Thinks his powder's getting closer." Following, Laine opened the cabinet. A neat array of instruments blinked up at him. "The old fool. He's nuttier than a fruit cake," and Drake turned away.

But Laine was lifting out the tray of tools. His hand passed over the smooth interior and its hinged top gently opened. Laine grinned at Drake's surprised face. He gestured toward the small silver dial.

"It's all yours, Junior. Do your Jimmie Valentine on it." Drake rubbed his fingertips swiftly over the cloth of his coat. He looked worried. He gave them another brisk rub and knelt before the cabinet. His face took on a dreamy look as he slowly, intently turned the knob. Back and forth, he twisted it, as gently as he'd stroke an infant's cheek. Laine watched the stubby fingers at work, turned sensitive as a surgeon's.

There came a small, dull click and Drake drew the safe drawer open.

"Ah," breathed Laine, "good boy."

Saffron colored fingers darted into the interior. A white hospital gown sped from the room, and a squeal went with it.

"The guy can run," said Drake when he was able to get his open mouth to work.

Laine took a step toward the doorway. "Yes. He's got his stuff." He stopped. "Oh, hell, let him go," and went back to the safe.

It contained a small sheaf of papers. "But I think they do the business," said Laine. "It covers Ten Eyck's transactions."

"They look kind of funny to me," said Drake over his shoulder, "Don't hardly make sense."

"Oh, it's a type of code, but from the looks of it, it can be broken easily enough."

They closed the safe and returned the instruments. "Neat," commented Laine. He looked around the room. "Well, let's go pick up Pop. He's probably in dreamland now. We'll dump him in some institution." He gazed quizzically at Drake. "You know he was a cop once?"

"Who? That coke snifter?"

Laine shrugged. "It takes all kinds. Some stay good. Some go bad. Just like people. Ten Eyck was no credit to the medical profession, either. But he went bad, there are still plenty of good ones left."

They found Pop quiet and sleeping. It was easier for them to dump him in the car and finish their night's work. Laine headed his car down the streets for home.

The sky was beginning to get light at six o'clock, but it was still only the flush of promise. Laine's face was haggard, a grey color from lack of sleep, with dark shadows beneath the eyes.

He dialed a number and sat down on the divan to wait. "Mrs. Barclay?" he said. "Didn't get you up, did I?" He laughed. "That's why I called. Thought those kids of yours were alarm clocks... Yes, this is Laine. The old man isn't stirring yet, is he?" He laughed again. "That's what I thought." He hunched over the phone wearily. "Well, I've been doing an all-night stint. Just got home... Listen, Mrs. Barclay, tell your husband to trot up here about nine o'clock. That'll give me three hours to sleep. I've got some dope to give him..."

Laine cradled the phone and dropped back against the pillow.

CHAPTER TWENTY-THREE

Barclay leaned against the door jamb watching Laine measure out the coffee.

"Loud pajamas you're wearin'," he observed. "Maybe you expected somebody more shapely than me?"

"I like 'em loud." Laine cracked an egg in the skillet. He looked up at Barclay. "Want an egg?"

"No. I had my breakfast. Just coffee. Gotta watch my waistline." Barclay patted his girth.

Laine laughed. "You should have watched that years ago. Too late now."

Barclay lounged in, leaned over the stove to feel the material of Laine's dressing gown between his finger and thumb. "Nice stuff," he said.

"Look out, you might get burned."

Barclay sat down and hunched a chair to the table. "You bachelors can afford to wear silk like that. We married men have a hard enough time gettin' money together for payments on the house," he sighed. "You oughtta see my bathrobe. An old flannel rag I've had for eight years. No glamour. The kids've always gotta have somethin'—tonsils jerked or piano lessons."

Laine flipped his egg to a plate and placed it on the table. "Stop grousing. Those kids'll always come first with you. You're a good father."

Barclay watched the hot coffee spout into the cup before him. "They won't think so if I don't get out and get 'em some Christmas presents pretty soon."

Laine sat at the table and buttered his toast. "Barnes turn up yet?"

"No. They're lookin' for him. We doubled the guard on the Thurmond place. If he's as nuts as I think he is, he'll go back there."

"How about her?" Laine watched Barclay.

"Mrs. Thurmond? I stopped around at the hospital this morning. They said she could have visitors now."

"Did you see her?"

"No. I figured that for your department."

"Good. I'll talk to her. Did Mockley get home last night?"

"About an hour after Mrs. Thurmond was slugged."

Slowly, Laine set his coffee cup down. "What did he say?"

"When the boys collared him and wanted to know where he'd been, he got real aristocratic with 'em. Said it wasn't any of their goddamned business in nice words."

Laine grinned. "Did they convince him it was their business?"

"In a way. They didn't peep about the Thurmond episode. They just said they were there to keep tab on him and he'd better open his yap." "Did he?"

Barclay finished his coffee while Laine waited. He wiped his lips delicately. "He said he was out drivin'."

"Just driving? No place in particular?"

"Just out for the air."

Laine pushed back from the table. "Sometimes I wonder if the automobile is such a boon to mankind as they would have us believe. You can always get in it and drive nowhere or get in it and drive somewhere—but say you were nowhere."

Laine lit a cigarette. Barclay watched him through the smoke. "You look kinda ratty today. Like you been out on an all-night toot."

"Didn't get in 'til six."

"That's what the wife said. What happened out there?"

Laine's face squirmed with the memory. "Well, Ten Eyck is no longer a murder suspect."

"You don't say. He had proof he wasn't in L.A. last Monday?"

"He had witnesses."

"Well, he coulda hired it done."

Laine dropped the cigarette to sizzle out in the bottom of the coffee cup. "We've still got some hot ones. We don't need to cast about for a hired killer."

"You favored Ten Eyck. I was just sympathisin'."

"Save your sympathy for Ten Eyck."

Barclay leaned forward, elbows on the table. "Why does he need sympathy?"

"He's dead."

"Oh." Barclay's impassive face showed nothing.

"You know," said Laine, "I drop a bombshell like that in your lap and you say 'oh' and don't look anything."

"It's the best way in this business. How'd he get it?"

"His wife." I guess she got tired of his racket on her money. When it looked like he'd have to start dodging the police, she just let him have it."

Laine tapped the table top with nervous fingers. "Shot him. Then she shot herself."

"Where were you?"

"In the kitchen. Talking to the maid."

"Pretty one, huh?"

Laine's face became stiff. "I wasn't talking to her because she was pretty. She was a witness to Ten Eyck's whereabouts on Monday. She's in the clear and she put him in the clear."

"Weren't you afraid of somethin' like that?"

"What? The shooting? No. Why would I?"

"Well, I guess you wouldn't. No. I guess not."

"I heard them quarrelling and I went down the hall to listen. I wanted to see if I could get some inside dope. A hot quarrel between husband and wife will bring out some cold truths every time."

"You're not kiddin'."

"But she only accused him of being in the baby-racket. Nothing specific. Then she let him have it."

"She musta worked fast if she shot herself, too, before you got to 'em."

"She did. By the time I could get my feet working and into the living room, she raised her gun and it was all over."

"So you didn't get anything out of the trip but a coupla bodies."

"Oh, yes I did." Laine rose and walked to the other room. He came back with the sheaf of papers. "I got this. Ten Eyck's transactions. This'll probably be the proof that'll tie Mockley and Mrs. Thurmond up with the Barnes baby."

Barclay looked it over. "It don't make sense," he said. "Don't even look like English."

"It's a code. But a simple one. I could decode it myself if I had the time."

"Oh." Barclay stared at the papers.

"You keep them. Take them down to the code room and get a good man on it."

"I didn't drive my car out here. Had one of the boys drop me off."

"Okay. I'll take you down, and go on to the hospital. Come in the living room and wait for me while I get dressed."

Barclay lay stretched out on the divan, hands beneath his head, his expressionless face pointed toward the ceiling. "Did you talk to any of the nurses out there?"

Laine's voice came from the open bedroom door. "He paid them off that night. He got rid of a couple of servants and dismantled the hospital. He worked fast. He probably figured I'd either come back with help or send someone out there. He must have known I was an officer."

"It don't show," said Barclay indulgently.

"Pop knew it."

"How about Pop? Was he among the missing?"

"He was there. Ten Eyck hadn't given him his shot and he was having the shakes."

"I've seen 'em."

"It was the first time Drake ever had, I think. He was fit to be tied."

"Well, I'm kinda sorry Ten Eyck's out of the picture," said Barclay thoughtfully. "I think he was the one for the gas chamber.

"I don't like to think of the gas chamber." Laine's voice was muffled.

Barclay sat up, folded his hands on his knees. "Don't you believe in capital punishment?"

"Well, I suppose it's the only way. An eye for an eye, a tooth for a tooth and a life for a life."Laine appeared in the doorway, smooth, dapper, but his face still holding its gray pallor.

"I don't think so much about it, Barclay, when I'm on the killer hunt. I just think about the poor devil the guy killed."

He walked over to the table, aimlessly moved about the few things it held. "Then when we get the killer by the seat of the pants and throw him in stir, and he signs a confession ..." Laine shook his head. "Then he's up against a first degree murder rap with nothing but the gas chamber to look forward to ... then, I don't know ... it bothers me." The minute the apartment door was locked, the telephone rang.

Laine looked at Barclay. "Two seconds later," he said, "and we'd have been down the steps. Wouldn't have heard it."

He stood there, wondering whether or not to go back and answer it. The phone ran angrily.

"Maybe it's a wrong number," he said carefully, "or someone asking for a donation."

"You can deduct donations from your income tax," said Barclay.

The phone gave three short, warning rings.

"Oh, hell." Laine unlocked the door and strode to the instrument.

"Laine talking," then he raised his eyebrows at Barclay and sat down to listen. Quietly, Barclay closed the door after himself and leaned against it.

"That's right, Mr. Turnbull," Laine said into the mouthpiece, a grin upturning the corners of his mouth. "Even if you are as innocent as a baby, it's better to tell us all about it. Then we, too, know you are as innocent as a baby." Barclay twirled his hat on his forefinger and crossed his legs.

Laine leaned over in a listening attitude. His face slowly twisted in anger. "She really wanted to marry you, then?" he asked, "On your terms." Slowly, he nodded. "Yes, I guess she was pretty crazy about the baby. After all, it was her baby..." Laine took a pencil from his pocket. He pulled an old envelope toward him and started to write.

Noiselessly, Barclay walked over. He looked down at the scribbling, hoping to get some clue to the conversation, and shook his head with disgust. Laine was doodling women's breasts again. Barclay paced the floor, easily and rhythmically.

"Okay, Turnbull," said Laine into the phone. "I've got that. Now, let's go back to the beginning and find out what kind of grounds went into the pot to make such swill..."

Barclay turned to look at him.

"Okay..." said Laine. He nodded, then shook his head. He drew a new pair of breasts and outlined a brassiere on them.

"I don't get it," said Laine, "did you love the girl or didn't you? Oh, I see... You had to have everything all nice and even like a problem in mathematics. Like an equation..." Laine hunched over the phone. "You know, Turnbull," he said confidentially, "there was an X slashed on her breast. Now you've been doing a lot of yammering about X being the unknown quantity."

Barclay could hear little sputterings through the receiver from where he stood. Laine looked up at him, his eyes blank.

"I know, Turnbull," he said, "but you could have figured another way to solve your problem... by doing away with the girl..." He nodded. "Yes," he agreed, "you have a point there. The baby still would have been in existence and loused up your pretty design..."

Laine allowed his body to slump with weariness. Two lines etched themselves from the corners of his mouth down to his jaws. "I don't blame the uncle for being sore. The brother, either. It was the trick of a first class heel."

Barclay was becoming impatient. He walked over to the window and looked out between the slats of the blinds as he teetered on the balls of his feet.

"Then you didn't see her after that. Right?" Laine leaned back against the pillows, the phone still at his ear. "Now about the brother," he said.

Barclay turned to watch him relaxed against the pillows. But his eyes were alert, his knuckles white on the phone. "Do you know where he lives?... oh ..."

Laine closed his eyes as he listened, but his fingers were still tight. He opened his eyes, flicked a glance at Barclay. "No, Turnbull," he said into the phone. "I'm afraid it won't be that easy for you. You'll have to come down to headquarters or we'll have a subpoena out for you..." Laine tapped a forefinger against the handle of the phone. "I don't believe you and I don't disbelieve you," he said. "You make that statement. Then we'll see."

He cradled the phone and cut off the sputter.

Leaning back again, against the pillows, he looked up at Barclay. "A literal mind," he said, "can be as illogical as a maze."

"What'd he say?" Barclay lounged over to drop into a chair. He pulled a cigarette from a rumpled package and lit it.

"Well," said Laine, settling the pillows more comfortably at his back, "I'll tell you. This Turnbull got Mary Barnes in trouble."

"Tch. Tch."

"He thinks that's his big mistake. Not because he didn't marry her and loused up her life, but because he got her in trouble and loused up his own pretty design."

"Maybe he couldn't marry her," suggested Barclay.

"He couldn't," answered Laine, "he had a mother."

"Hell, everybody has mothers. They get married anyway."

"Right. But he lived with his mother. That made a design. Mother and son. If a girl had come into the picture, it would've gotten lopsided. See?"

"No," said Barclay flatly, "I don't see. It happens all the time."

"Well, it doesn't happen to the Turnbulls." Laine tapped his front teeth with his fingernail. "Her uncle kicked her out when he found out what was happening… and her brother heaped all kinds of bad wishes on her. Turnbull probably convinced her she'd seduced him and took her to Dr. Ten Eyck."

"I don't get it," said Barclay stubbornly. "How come he was going to marry her now, then? The other all happened over three years ago."

"That's a good question," praised Laine. "After Turn-bull's mother died, he figured he was ready to make a new design out of his life, so he started looking for Mary. Seems he had a little trouble locating her. Her family had split up. She had dropped out of sight… probably got a job somewhere, slinging hash or something. So he advertised."

"He did, huh?"

"Probably had his ads running side by side so they'd be balanced or something silly like that. Anyway, he found her. So he told her that now he would marry her if she got the baby back."

Barclay leaned forward. "But the baby was adopted out. Why was it so important to get it back? He didn't want it in the first place."

Laine shook his head. "You just don't understand," he complained. "The baby was his and the girl's. If he married the girl and didn't have the baby, the design would be crooked. The books out of balance. The equation would always have an unknown quantity."

"Hell," said Barclay, "he killed her. Anybody that nuts would do anything."

"We all have our phobias," said Laine. "I have to put my right shoe on first in the morning. If I start with my left one, I take it off and start over again. Illogical, I know. But it's one of those things. I count stairs, too. I can tell you how many steps there are up to the City Hall. Or how many up Thurmond's terrace. How many there are up to the porch of the Parkway Hospital..."

"I don't do any of those things," said Barclay.

"Okay, you're normal. Or maybe you're the one that's nuts," grinned Laine.

Barclay frowned. "Does he know anything about the brother?"

Laine shook his head. "He hasn't seen him for more than three years. The girl hadn't, either, I guess, except for glimpses. She thought he always had a finger on her."

"Could be," said Barclay. "It could be Turnbull just said that to throw suspicion."

Laine nodded. "Turnbull decided to make a clean breast of things after he went to the party last night."

"What party?"

"The one the principal gave. Remember? He got to thinking of his position. They'd kick him out of school if this thing broke. He figured if he told me about it, we could bust it for him."

"I don't like the guy."

"I don't, either. If he wasn't all tied up with these dumb ideas, the girl would probably be alive. He and the girl and the baby would all be living out in the Valley somewhere..."

Impatiently, Laine stood.

"He was sure mixed up," said Barclay. "Its about the damndest thing I ever heard of."

"It isn't, either," corrected Laine. "You hear of crazy things all the time. People make up their own problems, then they walk right into them. They tie themselves up all nice and tight, then they holler for help, or kill somebody, or adopt a baby out or some damn fool thing."

CHAPTER TWENTY-FOUR

Laine kept his eyes on the clefted chin of the girl before him. "Dimple in the chin—devil within," ran through his mind.

He leaned an elbow on the desk and draped himself over it. "You know," he said, "there's something about a pretty girl in a nurse's uniform."

"That's what my husband always says."

Laine straightened. "You say the room is 187?"

"Yes. To your right and just past the turn."

"May we be left alone? Can the nurses with their thermometers and the interns with their good intentions be kept out while I'm there?"

"You want to be alone with her. Is that it?"

"Listen ... I just want to talk to the woman. I've got some questions to ask and I don't want to be bothered."

"Okay." The nurse glanced at her watch. "The luncheon trays won't be around for another hour. You won't be disturbed before then."

"Thanks. That's enough time." Laine moved away from the desk. He looked back. "Say 'hello' to your husband for me."

The door of 187 stood slightly ajar. Laine pushed it to walk in. He saw a bandaged head on a white-cased pillow. He closed the door softly behind him and stood by the bed.

"You don't look natural without your red hair showing," observed Laine.

"So you're here," she murmured.

Laine wriggled a small hollow at the side of the bed and settled himself.

"How are you feeling?"

"All right, I guess."

"You know who gave you those knock-out pops?"

"The hospital said I had an accident. I don't remember it."

"Did they say what kind of accident?"

"They said a car accident."

"It wasn't a car accident. Don't you remember parking the convertible and starting down the sidewalk?"

"Before your apartment? Yes. I remember that."

"Then you were out for the count. Somebody bopped you."

"Who did it?"

"That's what we want you to tell us."

She started to shake her head. Then she closed her eyes tightly to let the spinning furrows spread on her brow.

"So you were coming to see me?" Laine stared down at the copper-tipped eyelashes shadowing the pale cheek. "Why were you coming to see me?"

The eyes opened. The lashes curled back. "I thought you could help me."

"How?"

"Well, I was going to tell you something. Now, I think I'd better wait 'til I get well, 'til I feel like myself."

"And look better, huh? Well, Mrs. Thurmond, a woman as pretty as you can be quite appealing in bed, even if her red hair is all wound round with swaddling cloths." Laine's gray face had become harsh. "Spill it."

Mrs. Thurmond took a deep breath. "About Susan," she said, "You're right. She isn't mine."

"I know. She belonged to the Barnes girl, didn't she?"

"Yes. Somehow, that girl found out where her child was. She came to see me."

"And threatened you with exposure."

"Yes." Mrs. Thurmond's face flushed. Laine wondered if she would last out the interview. His eyes traveled to the bell cord. "But I didn't kill her to keep her quiet, Mr. Laine. You'll have to believe me."

"I don't have to believe anyone."

"I offered her money and she wouldn't take it."

"Real mothers want their babies," observed Laine, "money's a poor substitute."

"I didn't even know she was dead until Dr. Mockley told me."

"Maybe he killed her."

"Dr. Mockley?" Mrs. Thurmond smiled faintly. "No. He read it in the paper."

"Did he know she threatened you?"

"Yes."

"Well, that'd scare him. If you were found out, he would be too."

"He didn't kill her."

"How do you know?"

"I told you. He read about it in the paper."

Laine's face showed his disbelief.

"Can't you keep Susan out of this, Mr. Laine?"

"For your sake, not Susan's?"

"For Susan's sake. I'm all the mother she knows." A tear rolled down a smooth cheek. Laine wondered if she could do it by will power. "Susan will have every advantage. Would you take that away from her?"

"You mean, would I take all the money away from you which you got through Susan, don't you?"

"If I didn't have it, Susan wouldn't. Some day, she'll inherit the principle of a trust fund. If you bring this out, she won't have anything. She'll be turned over to some orphanage."

Laine mulled it over. He glanced down. Mrs. Thurmond was watching him.

"Susan's a pawn," he said wearily. "You need her to steal a trust fund. We'll have to use her to put it back." He stood up tiredly.

The woman's flushed face had grown mottled, the white patches gradually taking over the whole. Laine looked down at her. She closed her eyes.

"Did anyone know you were coming to see me last night?"

Her voice was a small breath of sound, dead, like her hopes. "Dr. Mockley knew. I told him I was going to throw myself on your mercy."

Laine moved impatiently. "You were going to try to deal with me. What'd he say?"

"He begged me not to. He became angry ..."

"I'll bet he did." Laine gazed at her speculatively. "Would you be willing to sign an affidavit so we can swear out a warrant for his arrest—assault and battery?"

"No." Now her face was dead white.

Laine leaned over and pushed the buzzer on the cord.

A nurse came almost immediately into the room.

"She doesn't look so good," said Laine. "Better 'tend to her."

"You've tired her out." The nurse bustled starchily toward the bed.

"Well, she can rest now. I'm leaving."

CHAPTER TWENTY-FIVE

"Barclay here?" asked Laine.

"He's in the code room. You guys got something good on that case?"

"Think so. Can I go back?"

"Sure. Go ahead. You know your way."

Laine started, then he stopped and turned, listening. The sound of a loud voice and laughter came drifting through the corridor, punctuated by pounding fists.

"What's out front?" asked Laine, "a drunk?"

The officer shrugged. "A character," he said, "some old cluck wants to make a statement."

"Wants to make one? Generally they dig in their heels to keep from making one."

"Well, this old duffer's anxious. He wants the world to know that he always did his duty. For my part, I don't think the world gives a damn."

"His duty, huh? Duty toward what?"

"His family. This's family trouble, I guess. Something in the paper or on the radio or something. He just wants us to know he didn't have anything to do with it."

Slowly, Laine retraced his steps. "Where is he?" he asked.

"Down there," the officer pointed. "Where the door's open. Go in, if you want to. It isn't private. We'll get him calmed down and kick him out."

Laine looked around the open door and into the room. The dust glistened like stars along the sunbeam which slanted through the window onto the fuzzy white hair and the weathered face of the old man. He was giving a speech and beating his fists against the top of an oak table. Two uniformed officers watched him. One sat in the windowsill, the other straddled a chair.

Laine gestured toward him, his words small against the tirade. "What's his name?"

"John Mentor," called one of the officers. "He's mad at somebody and wants to make a statement."

As Laine walked into the room, the old man turned. "It's a fine thing," he loudly complained, "when an honest man wants to talk and nobody listens ..." The officers laughed.

"Sit down," invited Laine. "I'll listen."

"Look here, Laine, if you think you can walk in here and tell us how to run our business ..."

"I think I can. I've been wanting to talk to this man."

"The old goof'll keep you all the rest of the day."

"So what?"

With a triumphant glance at the policemen, Mentor slid into a chair beside the table. "So you'll listen, huh?" he asked truculently.

"Sure, I'll listen."

"Well, all right, then. I pay my taxes. I mind the law. I don't see why those cops acted like I was something out of the funny paper."

"Maybe 'cause they're something out of the funny paper themselves."

"Wise guy," muttered one of the officers.

"You had something on the radio about a guy by the name of Barnes."

Laine nodded.

"From what the radio said, he sounded like my nephew."

"I think so."

"What's he done?" The old man leaned forth, his hands rigidly clasped.

"We don't know yet," said Laine, sidestepping the issue. "He was seen walking back and forth in front of a house ... acting in a suspicious manner."

Mentor snorted. "He always acted suspicious. That's nothin' new."

"But this was the house where Mary's baby lives."

"Mary's baby ..." the old man's face fell to pieces. "So she did have her baby." Looking around the room, he finally centered his attention on Laine. "Did that dirty scum who thought he was so all-fired smart marry the girl, then?"

"Turnbull? No," said Laine, "he didn't."

Mentor's mouth worked. He swallowed, trying to find the right words for a question.

"Mary had the baby," said Laine, "then she had it adopted out."

The old man stood up. He pounded the table with his fist, then he sank to the chair again. "She sold her own flesh and blood," he roared. "Turned away from it. I always thought maybe she was a good girl and I should've kept her on—her and her baby after it came. But she was no good. Why, I took her in and that fool brother of hers when they didn't have no home, and raised 'em. I did it 'cause they was my flesh and blood. But she turned away from hers."

"Let's not be harsh," said Laine softly, "she's dead, now."

"Dead? Who's dead?"

"Mary. She died a week ago."

The old man stared.

"She was killed. Murdered. It was right afterwards we caught your nephew prowling around that house."

The old man clamped his thin lips together. "I don't know nothin' about nothin'."

"Well, do you know where your nephew lives?"

"Ain't seen him for over three years. Don't know nothin' about him." Mentor's face closed up.

One of the officers gave a self conscious laugh. "Looks like he's finding out he doesn't want to talk so bad after all."

Laine sighed. "It does, at that." He noticed a relic of a typewriter on a stand in the corner. He looked at Mentor. "You don't know anything about this, then?"

The old man shook his head. Walking over, Laine seated himself before the typewriter. He opened a drawer and pulled out a piece of paper. He inserted it. "Where do you get these things?" he asked the officers, "from the dump?"

"That isn't one of our good typewriters. That one's put in here in case guys like you want to write 'Now is the time for all good men...'"

"Now is," said Laine. He looked over at Mentor.

"You say you know nothing about your nephew or your niece for the past three years?"

"Three and a half...mebbe almost four."

Laine tapped out the words.

"You know nothing about the birth of the baby? The adoption proceedings or anything like that?"

Mentor shook his head.

"Why did you come in to see us in answer to the radio appeal?"

The words were hard for the old man to follow. He thought them over. "If that nephew of mine," he finally decided, "was in some kind o' trouble, I wanted to tell you I'd done my best for him. I took care o' him and raised him." The old man's shoulders slumped. "I never wanted to, but he was kin, and I done my duty. I wanted to ask you people—you're the law—if I was through doin' my duty or if I had to take care o' him through this new trouble..."

Laine watched Mentor as he slumped before the table. The man was bewildered with these things he didn't understand. His shoulders too frail to carry a burden of decision.

"I think you did your duty," said Laine. He looked down at the words written on the white sheet of paper. "I hope," he said, "you didn't overstep it and mete out a punishment of your own…"

The old man's face was blank with perplexity.

"And I hope you've told us the truth."

When he gave his address, Laine mentally placed it about three blocks from the hotel where Mary Barnes had died. "What kind of a place is this?" he asked, "is it an apartment house, a hotel, or what…?"

"It's a shed behind an apartment house. I take care of the place."

Laine looked at him with new suspicion. "Mary died not far from where you live," he offered.

The old man stared at him, blank faced, secretively.

Laine sighed and pulled out the sheet of paper. He uncapped his fountain pen. "Sign this, please."

The knotted fingers held the pen awkwardly. They drew a wavering X at the bottom of the page.

"You can't write your name?" asked Laine.

Mentor shook his head.

Fingering his underlip, Laine hummed a little tuneless song. He looked over his shoulder at the officers. "There was an X on the girl's breasts," he said conversationally. "We've got a mathematician who's crazy about X's, a doctor whose middle initial is X and his last name's got a *ten* in it. Now an illiterate with the signature X. How do you like that?"

"Why'nt you lock this one up?" suggested one of the officers.

"Think I will," said Laine. "Figure out something on him. Take him in and book him. I'm going to start rounding them up. This damn case—" He strode from the room, and away from John Mentor's protestations.

CHAPTER TWENTY-SIX

Laine walked down the hallway and opened a door. Barclay looked up as he entered, but the code officer continued to write.

"How are you getting along with it?" Laine asked.

"Fine. I'll have it all ready for you tomorrow, and typed up."

"Good. It is a list of accounts, isn't it?"

"Sure is. Whatever it was must have been a profitable business."

"Oh, it was. While it lasted."

Laine turned to Barclay. "The deeper you go into this the deeper it gets."

"How was the redhead?"

"It doesn't show any more. All bandaged up." Laine perched on the side of the desk. "You were right. She was ready to deal."

"Yeah?"

"She turned on the tragedy—all about what would happen to the child if we exposed her. How she'd have to go to an orphanage maybe. I got to wondering. What will happen to her?"

"When this breaks open, the papers'll give it big stuff. Half of Los Angeles will want to adopt her."

"Maybe so. Tough, though, knocking a little girl around from pillar to post. Mockley was the one who banged Mrs. Thurmond."

"She knew it, huh?"

"No. I know it. He chased after her when he found out she was going to spill the beans to us."

"Well, it doesn't make him a murderer."

"It doesn't not make him a murderer, either."

Laine flicked a quick glance at Barclay. "I was just talking to John Mentor."

"Oh?"

"You can't even remember who John Mentor is."

"Am I supposed to?"

"Of course you're supposed to. Turnbull told us that was Barnes' uncle's name."

"Oh." Barclay sat up straight. "You talked to him? Here?"

"Right here. He came in to find out if the radio appeals were for his nephew."

"Yeah?"

"He wondered if he'd done his duty by rearing the kids or should he go through life and wet nurse them. He clammed up when I told him Mary Barnes had been killed. I can't be quite sure of him. He might have come to sound us out and establish his innocence. He might really be as dumb as he seems and come to see if he were responsible for Barnes."

Barclay shrugged.

"Anyway, he signed the statement with an X."

"Turnbull said he was illiterate—he couldn't read?"

"That could mean anything," said Laine. "It could mean the old boy didn't understand calculus. It could mean he couldn't write very well. I certainly didn't think it meant he couldn't even write his own name."

Laine twitched at the crease of his trousers and crossed his legs.

"The X kind of slugged me between the eyes. There're too many X's in this deal. We've got to start rounding them up before any more people kill any more people, or themselves, or get themselves conked on the noggin." The door opened. "Mr. Barclay."

Slowly, Barclay turned to look over the back of his chair. The chair squealed its protest.

"There's an old woman out here to see you. Says she thinks she's Barnes' landlady."

"Don't she know?" asked Barclay.

"Well, she thinks he's the one."

Barclay heaved himself up. "Probably another crackpot," he complained, "come on, Laine, let's listen to her."

She was a sparrow of a woman, perched on the edge of a hard chair, her brown coat neatly folded about her, her bright brown eyes busily interested. Her smooth gray-brown hair was caught in a tight wisp of braid and rolled into a marble-sized knot on her weatherbeaten neck. Her shirred lips over receded gums twisted up at the corners to give tidings that hers was a zestful life.

Laine paused in the doorway as Barclay approached her.

She shed her bright gaze upward. "Are you the man that wants to hear about Mr. Barnes?"

"I'd like to hear about him, yes ma'am." Barclay sat down beside her.

"But you don't have a policeman's uniform on. I was supposed to talk to a policeman."

Barclay took his badge from his coat pocket to display it gravely. "I'm a detective, ma'am."

"Oh, a detective." She jounced gleefully. "I have a Mr. Barnes who rooms with me."

"He lives with you in your home?"

"He has a room there. But he comes and goes."

"When was the last time he came and went?" asked Barclay.

She smiled happily. "Oh, I don't know. Every day is alike with me. Morning—noon and night and chickens. I have this extra room and Mr. Barnes uses it when he wants to. He helps me with the chores for his rent."

"You can't remember the last time you saw him?"

"It was a few days ago ..."

"Well, was it Sunday, Monday, or Tuesday?"

"I wouldn't know. The days are all the same out at my place. Just morning, noon and night and chickens..." she broke off abruptly. "But if everybody's looking for him, I'm worried about Mr. Barnes."

"We're worried about him, too, ma'am, if it's the same guy."

"Maybe he got run over," she volunteered. "He isn't a drinking man, but he doesn't always seem to have his wits about him. Maybe a hit-and-run driver ... the traffic is terrible. I don't like to come to the city myself, but I've never had an accident..."

"Did Mr. Barnes have a car, ma'am?"

"Oh, my no! He thought cars were tools of the devil. He didn't like it a bit when I had him come in to market with me. He said God gave us legs and we should use 'em."

Laine walked slowly into the room. The beady eyes took in his approach eagerly.

"Sounds like him," he murmured to Barclay. "What did this Mr. Barnes of yours look like, lady?"

"He was awful thin. He never did look like he had enough to eat, but I always fed him good out at my place. He was..." she stopped hesitantly, searching for description, then inspiration brought her neck forward and cocked her small head. "I saw a picture once of a man who went on a hunger-strike for some fool cause or another. I thought Mr. Barnes looked just like him."

Laine slipped his lower lip over his upper, caressing his hands together thoughtfully. "Perfect sketch of a fanatic. Better get her name and address, Barclay."

Barclay pulled out his notebook.

"Mary Etta Cording—Miss, that is."

"Address?"

"Oh, yes." Momentarily thrown off, she searched her mind for the numbers. "12321 Carter Way. It isn't a real street. That is, it just shows on the Engineer's Map. The city hasn't gotten around to putting the street in proper yet. Mine's the only house out there."

"Where is that, ma'am?"

"It's right before you get to the county line. It's near the wash. I'm practically in the wash, and sometimes it's pretty bad during the rainy season. I've got all my chicken pens up on stilts. They look like rabbit hutches..."

"Miss Cording," asked Laine, "how do you happen to be so late in reporting to headquarters? Mr. Barnes is no longer available for you to identify. We specifically urged in our news items and radio broadcasts, an immediate report."

The little woman's bright eyes became brighter with her rapid effort to explain. "I don't get a daily paper," she hurried, "the newsboys won't deliver out my way. I haven't a radio. I don't even have electricity. The city hasn't wired out that far, and I couldn't afford to have it brought out myself."

Laine shook his head at Barclay. "Sometimes it's so simple," he said wearily. "How did you learn of our appeal?" he asked the woman.

She folded her leathery hands in her brown lap in preparation of the recital. "Today is the day," she said in her happily excited lilt, "that I bring my chickens to market. The market manager asked where my helper was. Mr. Barnes often helped me with my chickens. That was the way he paid his rent. Well, when he asked where my helper was, I said, 'Mr. Barnes'? and he said, 'That guy that helps you unload'. The manager had to help me today and I guess he didn't like it."

Laine heaved a sigh and took one quick glance at Barclay's impassive features.

"Then all of a sudden, I guess the name 'Barnes' soaked in and the manager had about forty-'leven fits. That's when he told me I should go to the police."

"Fine," said Barclay.

"He said if it was the right Barnes, all of L. A. was looking for him. Is that right?"

"It's a little exaggerated. But we are interested."

"Why?" The woman's bright eyes were filled with concern. "Has he done something wrong? He was always quoting scripture and scolding the world for its sins. I don't think he'd do anything bad."

"We don't know whether he has or not," said Laine. "But we're trying to find him to be sure."

"Well, I hope he hasn't." She stood up, straightened her skirts. "Anyway, I've done my civic duty and I can't tell you where he is, because I don't know. I must get back to my chickens."

Briskly, she started toward the door.

"Just a minute, Miss Cording," called Laine, "we'd like to see this room of Barnes' if you don't mind."

"I don't mind. Although what you'll get out of it is more than I can see. I'll swan, all he's got in there is a few clothes and some mottos and books."

She opened the door.

"Wait," said Laine. "I wonder if you'd go out there with us?"

"Land, I've got my truck here. You can follow if you want to. But you'll have to hurry. I've got to get those chickens fed."

CHAPTER TWENTY-SEVEN

The sun, which had been lukewarm all day, shone hot and bright for its remaining few moments, like passionless senility in a desperate last fling. It was too early for homeward traffic, but harried shoppers still gutted the tinsel-gay streets.

Laine watched the signals and Barclay watched the pick-up they followed. The truck might have been its driver's lover, antiquated and patched, but still frolicsome.

"Think she can make it in that clunk?" asked Barclay.

"I'd have more faith in her heap than I have in my own. Know how much I paid for this bunch of chromium? Eighteen hundred smackers, and it's given me nothing but trouble." Laine banged the plastic steering wheel with his fist.

Barclay's eyes were still on their guide. "Looka that old girl go." He turned to Laine. "Did you see her run that light?"

"They drive like crazy—old people," said Laine tiredly. "So do kids." He thought a moment. "The ones in the middle do, too, I guess. But I'm scared to death of an old driver or a youngster on a bicycle. Gives me gooseflesh when I see them coming."

"We'll soon be out of this traffic." Laine's knuckles were white on the wheel. "Then we won't have to worry so."

"She'll prob'ly hit up such a pace then, the feathers will really fly."

Like a fine flurry of snow, the sailing white down before them indicated the truck's usual cargo.

They turned off on the broad highway. The truck centering the white line like a proud bride trailing her veil. Barclay watched the speedometer needle climb waveringly to fifty-five. "Where in hell are the traffic cops?" he complained. "We're in a thirty-five mile zone."

Small acreages sped by them, their packing box houses winged by framework, structures of the future.

Barclay took his eyes from the speedometer to say, "Lots of building going on 'way out here."

His eyes traveled back to watch the needle hover to sixty. "What a woman," he breathed, "if she isn't yackety-yacking, she's drivin' like a bat out of hell."

"She turned," said Laine. "My God!" The cloud of dust was a miniature cyclone. "Must have done it on two wheels." Laine slowed to make the curve, then speeded to keep the truck in sight. "I've never been out here. Have you?"

"No. But we're close to the wash, now." The road had become unkempt, and the little houses which blazed their owners' future hopes were gone. Burned-off hills with the courage of struggling sagebrush made up the scenery on each side of a road which had narrowed to a weed-grown lane, paved with variable stones.

"Gettin' rocky," observed Barclay. "The beginning of the wash."

In a sudden slither and clash of pebbles, the truck halted. Laine turned aside and put on his brakes.

Barclay stepped out.

Laine sat there, gathering his scattered nerves. He picked his way carefully from the car, to find his legs had become elastic. A sudden sense of the ludicrous and a feeling of resentment clashed within him.

He strode toward the little bird-like woman who was standing by her truck, unconcerned and unruffled.

"Listen, Lady," he said, "you just about broke every traffic regulation in the book getting us out here."

Her confused face looked up at him, to become indignant. "Young man, I've been driving for many a year now, and I've never had an accident."

"Yes, and I've seen people get their heads knocked off for half of what I saw you do today." Laine ticked the errors on his fingers. "First, you ran a light, then you didn't stop at a pedestrian crossing. You straddled the white line all the way down the highway, and you exceeded the speed limit like a hot rodder."

"You mean I did those things wrong?"

"Yes, lady. Those few I mentioned. Maybe there were others, too. But for my own safety and the safety of other drivers, I was trying to keep my eyes on the road." He looked down at her in wonder. "St. Christopher must be taking care of you."

Her little brown face wrinkled into a map of distress.

Laine patted her shoulder. "Never mind. Nothing happened." He became stern again. "But I'm going to send you a book of traffic regulations and I want you to read it."

He looked around. "This your place?" A windbreak of eucalyptus hemmed in the property. Laine walked over the sheets of bark they had discarded, the dry leaves they had shed. He saw a small vegetable garden struggling against the sand and shale, the long-legged chicken coops with their clucking contentment and the silver-aged cottage as beaten and unbowed as its owner.

"I must feed my chickens now." Miss Cording spoke directly to Barclay, making a wide circle around Laine.

"Could we see Barnes' room first?" asked Laine. "We won't disturb anything. You can do your feeding while we look around."

Silently, she led them to the house.

"She acts like a reprimanded school-girl," said Laine softly to Barclay.

"You hurt her feelings."

Through an antiquated parlor, shabbily tidy in its Victorian dress, she led them to a dark little room with one many-paned window looking out onto hazy evening. She struck a match to bring into pallid light an oil lamp which flickered the room into distortion.

"Before it gets dark," she said, "I'll have to feed those ..." and was gone from the room, her words trailing behind. By the lamp lay a wooden box. Laine placed his hand on it for support as he looked over the arid personality of the table top.

Barclay opened the small closet door. Expertly, he rifled the clothing. He turned over shoes to shake them in mid-air.

"What are you looking for?" asked Laine.

"I dunno."

"What did you find?"

"Coupla dirty handkerchiefs." Barclay closed the door with a bang.

"Take a look at the mottos on the wall," suggested Laine.

Barclay stared about and whistled. Over his head, a faded sampler hinted that this was "Home Sweet Home". It was done in childish stitchery, sloping and inaccurate.

"That, I have an idea," said Laine, "is Miss Cording's own." His hand waved the room. "The rest, I should judge, belong to Barnes."

Heavy black letters proclaiming that "The Wages of Sin is Death", blared its omen upon a background of white.

From a magazine, or perhaps a book, quotations had been clipped to be secured to the wall by small pieces of scotch tape. In soldierly row, they marched:

"Who can find a virtuous woman? For her price is far above rubies."

"The world, the flesh and the devil."

"This one's from Shelley," said Laine, reading: "'Music, when soft voices die, vibrates in the memory'."

Laine moved to stand before a piece of framed brown cardboard. "And this," he said slowly, "is turned toward the wall."

Barclay followed to look over his shoulder.

Carefully, Laine lifted the wire loop from its nail. He turned it and hung it up again. He read: "'My Sister! My Sweet Sister! If a name dearer and purer were, it should be thine.—Byron'."

"He didn't like that one, I guess," said Barclay. He turned to the drawers of the dresser. Piece by piece, he laid the few garments aside. "Not many clothes," he said. "No papers. No letters."

Laine stepped to a chair upon which a small pile of books rested.

He held them up to read their titles by the flickering light of the lamp. "A couple of volumes of Poe," he murmured, "A prayerbook and a book of Schopenhauer." This last, he held in his hand contemplatively. "A strange collection ... yet, maybe not so strange after all."

"You say something?" asked Barclay as he lifted dust papers from the drawers.

"Schopenhauer was gloomy, cynical—suspicious."

"He was?" Barclay laid the folded clothing back where he had found it.

"He had a paranoiac sense of unacknowledged genius. It comes out in his essays."

Barclay closed the drawer and turned.

"His philosophy shows a shame at continuing the race. To him, a woman was a shrew and a sinner."

"To who? Barnes?"

Laine smiled. He laid the book with the others. "To Barnes, yes. Didn't find anything, did you?"

"No. There's nothin' here to find."

Laine walked to the lamp and placed the palm of his hand on the box as he again surveyed the room. The feel of the wood finally made its presence known to him and he looked downward. Slowly, he opened the hinged top of the box and saw a record still upon its spindle, the arm just above, ready to send forth the music.

Barclay looked over his shoulder. "That's an old timer," he said. "Haven't seen one of those for a coon's age. Portable windup job."

"I never thought of a phonograph," said Laine with wonder. "All I could think of was a radio. Like the woman said—a radio."

"It don't really mean anything, though," said Barclay, "Since his landlady don't know when he left this room. Maybe the music box was sittin' here just as innocent Monday night."

"Maybe so."

Miss Cording appeared in the doorway. "You messing up any of Mr. Barnes' things?" she asked. The chickens seemed to have smoothed down her hurt feelings and returned her zest.

"No."

"What should I tell him if he comes back? Should I tell him you're looking for him?"

Laine whirled. "Barclay," he snapped. "Take my car and go down to that filling station on the highway. Call headquarters and tell them to send out a couple of men from the precinct station. I want 'em to pick off Barnes in case he should come back here."

Barclay brushed past the landlady and out of the house.

"You mean those men are coming here?" she asked.

"They won't bother you," said Laine. "They'll be outdoors some place. You probably won't even know they're here."

"But it will be cold tonight. Those poor men could come in here where it's warm. They could wait for Mr. Barnes in the house." Her brown clawlike hand slowly crept to the shirred lips. "What's Mr. Barnes done?" she asked, "What's he done that you're having men wait for him? He hasn't killed anybody, has he?" The last words were whispered tremulo.

"We don't know, Miss Cording. Maybe not. Several people had a motive, but Barnes had the personality. We just don't know."

The fear was still in her eyes, resting there incongruously in the brightness.

"You're not to worry. You'll be safe. Even without the cops, you'd be safe—and with them, it'll be like a sanctuary here." He turned to the box once more. "Do you remember seeing Barnes take this out of the house at any time?"

"That victrola? No. But I hardly ever come in this room. And sometimes I don't see him leave or come back, either. He takes a notion to wander off almost any time, middle of the night or middle of the day."

"Did he ever receive any mail?"

"Once. He burned the letter right up."

"When was that?"

"Not long ago. A few days, perhaps. I lose track of time."

"Did he ever mention a sister?"

"No." Mechanically, her eyes turned toward the motto. "You turned it back. That's nice, but he won't like it."

"When did he turn its face toward the wall?"

"It's always been like that. When he moved in here, he hung it up that way. I thought it was a mistake. I turned it around and he told me I must never touch it again."

"How long has he lived with you?"

"He moved in, oh, about a year ago. I forget time. Every day is just like another ..."

"Yes," agreed Laine.

He leaned over the box, wound it and started the disc to whirl. He placed the needle and sonorous organ music, scratchy with age and wheezy with out-dated mechanism, burst forth in startled obsolescence.

Miss Cording's twisted face turned from the hypnotic spiral of the record to Laine. "It's kinda sad, isn't it?"

Laine's eyes showed a discomfort deeper than the symphony of sorrow.

"I like gay music myself," she pled.

He switched the sound off. "I, too, prefer it."

Miss Cording smiled in the silence. "You know," she confided, "when Mr. Barnes used to get that thing going, I'd just go out and sit in the woodshed. I couldn't stand it. He doesn't have many records and they're all like that; not happy songs like I used to sing in church. But sad or cruel. They made me feel like a sinner. Happy hymns make you feel like you're not so bad and you'll try to do better."

"Yes," agreed Laine. He smiled down at her gently. "I think you've got something there."

He heard a car drive up and the front door slam.

Barclay said, as he entered the bedroom, "I waited for 'em at the filling station. They're outside now."

"Those poor men." Miss Cording bustled without moving from the spot. "You tell them to come right in for a nice hot cup of coffee."

"I'll tell 'em when we leave, ma'am. They'll appreciate it. Laine…"

"Yes?"

"When I called headquarters, they told me Mrs. Thurmond had signed an affidavit requesting the arrest of Dr. Mockley."

Laine's eyebrows rose. "On what charges?"

"Assault and battery with intent to kill."

"Hmm." Laine carefully closed the top of the phonograph. "Wonder what that means?"

"Well, I guess it means she knows he conked her."

"Maybe. Or it might mean she knows he killed Mary Barnes and she's scared of her own life. It might mean she killed Mary Barnes and is trying to get him in a spot where he'll have to take the rap."

"Anyway, they're on their way with the warrant now."

Laine examined the lower tray of the box. The edges of a sparse record collection lay darkly within. He picked the box up in his arms and started for the door.

"Are you taking it away?" asked Miss Cording.

"Yes. I'm taking it away."

"We didn't find much here, did we?" asked Barclay. Laine stared at him, surprised. He turned, his arms full of the box, to survey the room with its guttering shadows. "We found the essential Barnes," he said. "The books are his dogma, the mottos his creed." Lifting the box higher, he cradled it. "This music could be the execution of his principles."

He walked out of the house then and into the rapid cold of the night.

CHAPTER TWENTY-EIGHT

They rolled into a city crowded with cars and burdened shoppers, raucous with impatient horns and traffic whistles, bright with clustered lights and reflected color.

Laine rested against the steering wheel as congested traffic formed a line of inertia with its rare bursts of movement. "Almost nine o'clock. We would hit the worst of it."

Barclay sat in brooding silence, the box on his knees. Laine knew he was visualizing depleted toy shelves. He watched him during a deadlock of the traffic snarl, watched him work up a slow burn. His placid face showed none of the casting about for a convenient wrath objective, it showed only in the gradual unrelaxing of his body.

"Why couldn't we have gone home for dinner?" Barclay said. "My wife told me, over the phone, we had steak. She said there was enough for you." He chewed over the discontent in his mind. "But, no. You had to go to some greasy spoon and grab a sandwich ..."

Laine pulled the motor out of an idle and jumped forward ten feet. "I told you," he said, resting again, "we didn't have time to drive 'way out there. And we would have had to talk for awhile. We've got more important things to do."

Laine made a right-hand turn, to drive up a shadowed street, the noise of confusion fading behind him. Barclay patted his paunch. "But that kind of food isn't good for me. I can feel it settin' right here. Hard as a rock." Laine chuckled.

"I'll prob'ly have indigestion tonight. Keep me awake."

Laine pulled up in front of headquarters. "Think about the case, then," he said unfeelingly. "See if you can draw some conclusions." He stepped to the curbing. "Give me the record player. Be careful of it."

Barclay handed it over. "You act as if it had the crown jewels in it. I been babyin' this thing ever since we left that chicken ranch."

"I want to look it over."

"For fingerprints?"

"That's not good. They'd just be Barnes'. No. I want to look it over, and play with it, and think."

They walked up the steps and into the lighted foyer. A uniformed policeman lounged against the desk, talking to the sergeant. Laine placed the box on the desk.

"Whatcha got there?" asked the sergeant. "A Christmas present?"

Laine placed the handle in its side and twisted it tight. "Might be," he mumbled. "Might be, at that." He opened the top and started the disc.

"An antique," observed the sergeant.

Laine touched the needle to the record and placed his elbows on the desk to listen.

Organ muzic wheezed forth in a sniffling, strident camouflage.

"What kinda jive is that?" asked the policeman.

The sergeant grinned. "Why heck, don'tcha know anything? That's the new progressive jazz the kids are ravin' over. It's be-bop-rock-'n-roll…"

The policeman walked to the other end of the room. "Well, I like my music sweet and swingy."

"You're a modernist," said the sergeant. "With Laine, here, what was good enough for his father is good enough for him. If pop could stand those old cough boxes, so can he."

Laine switched the record still. "You boys don't realize it," he said, "but this box may be an influential piece of evidence."

"Listen," sneered the sergeant. "If you play that thing in front of a jury, they'll probably stick you in the prisoner's seat."

Laine turned to Barclay. "Let's take this where we won't have any hecklers. How about the code room?"

"Oh no, you don't," said the sergeant. "It's locked. You think we leave it open so every Tom, Dick and Harry from the Sheriff's Office can stick his nose in?"

Laine cradled the box in his arms.

"Come on," said Barclay. "I'll find a spot." He turned to the sergeant. "I guess you don't know we're on an important case."

"Yeah. I heard that. Must be important to let a star suspect vanish in thin air."

Laine and Barclay started down the hall. They turned, as the entrance door opened. Two officers walked through. "Barclay," called one, "we got your man Mockley in stir."

Barclay and Laine re-entered the room. Laine rested the box against the desk. "What did he say?"

"He said the whole thing was fantastic," the officer turned to his companion. "Wasn't that what he said?" The other nodded.

"He said the police department would look like a bunch of clowns before he was through." He turned. "Didn't he?" The nod again answered him.

"I feel real bad. He called us 'hoodlums'."

Laine chuckled. "Maybe you are. What did you do to him?"

The officer's face turned bland. "Us? Why, we didn't scramble him up none. We just shook him a coupla times." The officer looked hurt. "He wiggled and kicked. I feel like I been through a mixmaster. Don't you?" he inquired of his companion. The other nodded.

"He's screamin' for his lawyer. I told him he could get one in the morning. I said mouthpieces were hard workin' babies.

Sometimes, I said, they worked almost as hard as cops. And they needed their rest at night. We left him in the pokey yellin' 'injustice' and 'politics'."

Laine picked up his box and he and Barclay again headed down the hall.

Barclay pushed open a door. "Here. You can play it in here."

Laine placed the box on the table and took off his coat. He flipped the lever while Barclay watched in silence. The organ music threaded through the small slats and Barclay walked disconsolately to the window to sit upon the sill and stare out at the dark night.

Laine hovered over the spinning circle. The sonorous music became a wail in the room, to settle down in a repetitious monotony of angry chords. With startling suddenness, an alto voice broke through to master and reach over the sound of the organ.

Barclay whirled and Laine bent closer. In a room where suspects were questioned—in a room where men talked away their freedom and others talked their way to it, the voice rose in reedy slenderness through the apertures of the box.

"What can wash away the sin ..." the voice intoned, "Nothing but the blood—the blood—the blood—the blood ...."

"Turn it off!" yelled Barclay.

Laine switched the noise to silence. He looked at Barclay standing before the black window. "Jeez," said Barclay, "what is that thing?"

"It's a hymn." Laine released the record from its spindle. He held it up to the light. "And it's cracked."

"Sure is."

"It's cracked," repeated Laine slowly, "like someone was in a hurry to turn it off."

"Don't blame 'em."

"Like maybe they wanted to get out of where they were but fast."

Laine squinted at the old label. "The name of it's 'Nothing but the Blood'."

"You don't say," said Barclay.

Laine laid the record carefully aside. He knelt to the dusty floor and gently removed the collection from its shelf. He turned each record, reading closely. "They're all hymns," he said. "I never heard of any of 'em."

"Maybe you ought to go to church more often."

"Listen. I was reared in church. Our church didn't have these. We sang happy hymns." He thought of Miss Cording. "All these are sad or avenging." He piled the records by the side of the cracked disc.

Still kneeling, he wedged the flat of his hand in the now empty crevice. He jerked it out, red from the pressure, and stood to carefully slant the box. Out of the record slot slid a key. It came to rest on the table between Laine and Barclay's startled gaze.

CHAPTER TWENTY-NINE

"It's almost ten o'clock," said Barclay. "Maybe she won't be up."

Laine hesitated on the curbing and stared at him. "Are you kidding? These are her working hours."

"How you talk," murmured Barclay.

The ROOMS sign flickered a slack welcome, which was refuted by the close scent of the lobby.

"Phew," said Barclay.

"These people don't notice." Laine trundled his box to the desk. The mouse-faced clerk stared at them without comprehension, then suddenly his lips parted, his two long front teeth granting them recognition.

"That's the box," he said coming out of his slough of sluggishness. "The one I seen that night." He let disillusionment rest heavily upon Laine. "He didn't have it wrapped in no paper. He carried it just like that."

"You're sure of it?"

"As sure as I am that I'm standin' here."

Laine took in the sloping body, sagged against the counter. "How about the other two I described—the red-headed woman and the man with gray hair. You said you saw them that night, too."

"Maybe I did—you could go over them?"

"No. It would be putting words in your mouth. That woman who complained of the radio music the night of the murder—the one who had the room next to the girl's—she in?"

The clerk placed a grimy finger before his lips. "I think so."

"We'd like to see her …"

The clerk looked surprised. "Okay. Go up and rap on her door and go in."

"You don't stand much on formality in this flophouse, do you?"

"Huh?"

"Skip it. Come on, Barclay."

Laine hesitated before the gilt-spotted elevator. Barclay lumbered for the stairs. "You don't catch me in that mouse trap," he said. "I don't want to wake up and find myself dead in the basement."

Laine followed.

"This place stinks," said Barclay, when they reached the second floor.

"Dirty people. Dirty surroundings. It doesn't add up to Chanel Number Five. Here it is." Laine rapped on the streaked door.

"Yeah?" The voice slashed through the wooden partition to stab his eardrums.

"We want to have a little talk with you."

"What about?"

Laine turned to Barclay. "I always feel like a damn fool talking to a door," then louder, "I'm from the Sheriff's Office. We want to ask you about your complaint the night of the murder."

Abruptly, the door opened. Laine's fingers tightened on the box.

"You ain't gonna get me mixed up in no murder rap." The words spilled out spiced with whisky. The woman clutched with one hand a dirty pink wrapper about her pendulous breasts; the other was busy with metallic bronze hair. Then she saw Barclay. "Hello-o-o-o, there …"

"Jeez."

Laine gave Barclay a wicked sidelong glance.

"Come in," invited the woman, her hand growing listless on the wrapper front. "Come over and rest on the bed."

Barclay moved toward the window, planting himself squarely.

"You rest on the bed," Laine sternly commanded the woman. "I want you to listen to something."

She flounced upon a soiled gray-white counterpane, her smeared lips showing dissatisfaction.

"Now," said Laine more gently, "I understand you complained of the music next door the night of the murder."

"Yeah," she said sulkily, "it damn near drove me nuts. A bunch o' caterwaulin' if I ever heard any. Where anyone could find such a station—and they tuned it in on all the static on the air waves."

Laine opened up the box.

"Maybe it wasn't a radio," he said, "maybe it was this…"

Carefully, he placed the needle close to the crack. He switched the lever and a slow moving wail gave over, gaining in tempo as the disc swung into movement.

He watched the woman on the bed.

She stiffened, her hand dropping from the pink fabric it had held.

The music ground out, then with that staccato abruptness, the voice broke with the organ… "What can wash away the sin? Nothing but the blood—the blood—the blood—the blood…"

"Turn it off!"

Laine silenced the aria.

"That was it." The woman was staring at the box as if it harbored a coiled reptile. She smiled, a little shakily. "Kinda get you, don't it?"

"That was what you heard, then?" asked Laine, snapping the box shut.

"Gawd, yes. And I ain't forgettin' it."

"That's all." Again Laine cradled the box while Barclay opened the door to step out before him.

Contemplatively, Laine stood before the neighboring room. He set the box to the floor. He dragged the key from his pocket and turned it over and over on his palm. Then he stooped to insert it, gave it a twist and opened the door.

"I'll be goddamned. Where do you think you are?"

"In the wrong room, lady. In the wrong room. Sorry."

Laine banged the door closed, dropped the key in his pocket and picked up the box.

"It all fits, don't it?" said Barclay as they walked down the stairs.

"Seems to," agreed Laine. He stopped on the step. "Except I'm worried about the Thurmond-Mockley deal. It doesn't add. Why the arrest?"

CHAPTER THIRTY

The code officer looked myopically up. His eyes suggested that the distance from cryptography to anthropology was too great. They focussed at last.

"Oh. Here's that report, Laine."

"Thanks." Laine took the sheaf of papers. "All typed and ready."

"And here's the original."

Laine placed the two together. "They're evidence, maybe."

"Want to sit down and look it over?"

"Thanks. I will."

Laine sat in a leather chair by the window, the afternoon sunshine filtering wintrily over the pages. He turned the sheets until he reached the account which stopped him and set him to concentrated reading.

It was the second call of his name that lifted his gaze.

"Laine." Barclay lounged against the window. "Mrs. Thurmond is ready to leave the hospital."

Laine placed the papers on his knee. "She is?"

"Yeah. They won't let her go home without she's with an officer. Since we know so much about her, and she figures her immediate future is well mapped by the police, we're scared she'll climb a telephone pole."

"That isn't her brand of nerve."

"I think you'd better go down and get her. She's been yours all the way through."

"In a minute I will. Sit down."

"I see you've got the code all fixed up."

"Yes. And that fixed Mrs. Thurmond up nice and tight, too. And Mockley."

"Okay." Barclay folded his arms.

"Ten Eyck sold the Mary Barnes baby to Mockley for delivery to Thurmond."

"It shows there, in black and white, huh?"

"It does. Everything's dated nice and ship-shape, too. And here's the pay-off, the thing that not only ties Thurmond and Mockley into the racket, but knits 'em forever and ever—or at least as long as Ten Eyck had anything to say about it."

"And he hasn't, now."

"No. When he was killed, it lessened both Thurmond and Mockley's bills for the time being."

"You mean blackmail?"

"That's it. That devil Ten Eyck wouldn't let anyone go once he got his fingers on them. He got in a nice monthly income from both the redhead and the doctor."

"Wonder why they kept payin' him off? He couldn't open his yap about it, anyway, without stickin' his foot in."

Laine shrugged. "Well, they weren't taking any chances on it. They paid."

"What was the Barnes baby priced at?"

"What do you think?"

Barclay gazed out of the window in inexpressive thought. "Ten thousand?" he hazarded.

Laine grinned. "Chicken feed," he said. "No. That baby came high. Fifty thousand berries high. After Mockley was paid off and all the monthly contributions, she must weigh up to between one hundred and a hundred and fifty thousand dollars."

Barclay whistled.

Laine stood. "So now I've got to go out and get the redhead and escort her home. "You know," he looked at Barclay thoughtfully, "a pretty woman without ethics is like a rosy apple with a worm in it. You smack your lips over it and you enjoy it until you come to that wriggling, slimy, soft body. Then, when you throw the rest of the apple away, you don't remember how round it was, how juicy and how tartly sweet, you just remember its contamination."

CHAPTER THIRTY-ONE

To Laine, the veneer appeared splotchy. "Like a sloppy paint remover job on hard enamel," he thought.

She looked just the same; the red, copper-tipped hair spraying from the saucy, bandage-concealing hat, the slim, curved body a cryptic revelation within the smart, well-cut frock.

She had stepped from peasantry to peerage, and Laine was watching her step back again, regretful, and afraid of the future, but no longer tight-drawn and watchful. When her mind momentarily grasped the thought of what might be, Laine could sense the panic squeal in her breast.

"They tell me," she said, looking out the window, her cameo profile facing Laine, "that I'm not well enough to drive home. But they also tell me, when I suggest calling a taxi, that I will be provided a way home. So I knew I would be escorted under guard and I figured the guard would be you." She faced Laine.

"I hope you're not too disappointed."

"Not particularly. I just don't want to go home. Not out there to listen to the patter of baby feet that got me into this goddamned mess."

"Where did you want to go?"

"Oh, almost anyplace else. Palm Springs, maybe—Las Vegas. Somewhere I could have a good time. Somewhere I could forget my troubles."

"And latch onto another marriage—another fortune?"

"Maybe."

"Well, Las Vegas or Palm Springs, too, would be a little out of the way. The police wouldn't like it."

"I suppose not."

She took a step toward him. "What do you think they'll do to me?"

"They don't know yet whether you illegally adopted a baby to steal an income or whether you're a killer."

"Well, when they find out I'm no killer, then what?"

Laine shrugged. "I'm a homicide man, myself. Baby juggling and larceny's out of my line."

"Damn." She whirled to the window again. "Everybody's so cockeyed close mouthed. I can't make any plans. I can't figure my next move."

"The next move is not up to you. You can't do anything. You've been close mouthed yourself. Don't gripe about other people. You'll go home and you'll sit and you'll wait until something's decided. That won't be long. I've got the proof at headquarters now about you and Mockley. It's out of my hands. Don't be impatient with the home you worked so hard for, or the patter of little feet. You won't be there long, and you won't be listening to the patter long. You might be sitting in a nice little private cell all of your own tonight, listening to the beat of a warder's feet. And don't protest about it, either. You worked for that, too. You worked for it just as surely as you worked for the other."

She stared at him, open-mouthed.

"You didn't really expect it, did you? You knew it might happen, but you didn't figure it could happen to you."

"I'll get a lawyer."

Laine looked weary. "That's up to you. You can get a lawyer right away if you want to. You can call one now. Or you can phone when I get you home. I don't care."

He saw the same washed-out pallor come into her face which had drained it of its unhealthy flush while in bed, during their last interview. He saw her lose hope again. He knew that this girl as long as she lived, would raise and lower her hopes, as help came to her and was then withdrawn.

"Why did you have Dr. Mockley arrested?" he asked suddenly. "You refused to sign an affidavit when I asked you to."

He thought she wouldn't answer, she was quiet for so long. "He warned me," she finally said, "that if I blabbed about the baby transaction, he had a way out." She spread her hands in a gesture of final futility. "I kept brooding about it. If he did have a loophole, then I was left holding the bag. I don't want to hold it alone." Her voice turned to a whisper. "If it were a bluff, maybe he'd lay for me and kill me. Then I couldn't testify against him." Her face hardened. "I wanted him where he is now. In jail."

Laine's eyes watched her. "Maybe," he agreed, "maybe that's how it is. That's how your mind would work. And maybe you two were in on the killing—and you're fixing it so he'll get the heavy end."

He picked up the coat from the chair.

"Get into this," he commanded.

The mink in his hands was as soft as a baby's skin.

The sky which had been growing moody during the afternoon, now settled into a deep sullenness drawing the gray curtain of its temper over the cool light of the sun. Dark edges of its further discontent were creeping out fuzzily in warning of increased black wrath.

As Laine, through the half-light, rolled closer to the Thurmond estate, he couldn't help but wonder how many fake jewels were placed in the fine setting of this highly restricted neighborhood. He cast a sidelong glance at his partner on the seat. She might have been a social leader, homeward bound from a favorite charity drive. She might have been a servant girl back to the dishes after a day out.

The house on the knoll looked down disdainfully aloof under the darkening sky; its sheets of plate glass, blind eyes giving forth no recognition, shedding no welcome. The house was a dowager who had discovered its interloper.

Laine turned off the motor and looked at his companion. She, too, felt the rebuff of the house, not with a tiptoeing abashment, but with the dull boot-beat of sullen resentment.

Her mouth pouted, the outthrust lip of a sulky child in anger at the upset plans of the maturely vicious. "I don't want to go in there."

Laine sighed. "Well, you're going. I've had my orders. I'm giving you yours."

A tap on the window turned his eyes outward. He rolled down the glass.

The officer outside looked confused, a little frustrated. "Mr. Laine," he said, "I thought I saw someone prowlin' around here. I got out of the car to have a look-see, and I'll be damned if I can find a thing wrong."

"Don't you know whether you saw someone or not?"

The officer waved a hand in explanation. "In this light? A shadow might be anything. It's gonna rain cats and dogs inside of an hour."

"Well, is the gate locked?"

"Yeah. I checked that." The officer pointed toward the hollow tile wall, the double open centers of which were set on end forming a lattice effect, peep holes from the outside to the in. "I thought I saw something move along there. With the vines and the shadows of the trees, I ain't quite sure."

"Well," Laine nudged the officer aside and opened the car door. "I'm going in there. You stay outside and keep an eye open. If anything acts funny, grab it." He turned to the woman. "Come on."

He stopped at the gate. "You have a key?"

She shook her head, standing a little away from him, isolated, wrapped in self pity. "Ring the bell," she said coldly.

Laine pushed a button. He could hear nothing. He hoped it was wired to the house and in working order. He shivered, a mean little puff of wind with ice cold fingers had wrapped its way around his legs. It skittered away and rose with added strength and venom, to chatter the leaves and bend the branches of the trees.

Above the low wall of the terrace around the house and in the distance, Laine saw the door open to let out an oblong of light. The light continued to shine as he heard running footsteps down the flagstone walk.

The pallid color of the maid's uniform was a blurred outline as it neared the gate. She peered through the lacy ironwork. "Oh, it's you, Mrs. Thurmond." Her fingers fumbled at the lock, her tongue mumbled with embarrassment. "I didn't know you were coming home today, Mrs. Thurmond. If I'd only known. It's all the rest of the servants' day out. I'm here by myself. Me and Susan. Really, I haven't much fixed to eat…" She pulled the gate open, bracing herself against it as the wind rose to wrest it from her.

Laine nudged Mrs. Thurmond through and pushed the gates closed. They clicked with finality. Laine looked through at the deeper shadow of the officer's prowling.

He followed the women up the walk. He could hear the maid, "Are you feeling all right, Mrs. Thurmond? I'm so glad you're well again. But I'll have to get you a pick-up dinner. It's too bad. Would you like some hot tea now?"

He felt sorry for the maid as nothing helped her tripping words. Then he became impatiently irked. Why couldn't the fool girl shut her mouth—there she was—starting all over again with her regrets….

They walked up the steps of the terrace, behind the low stone wall and into the still open door. Laine closed it and waited for the warmth of the house to creep through his outer layers of clothing and lay hands on his chilled body.

But even when he knew he should be warm, he felt cold. It was the still face of Mrs. Thurmond, icy with ill-temper. It was the thought of the little girl in this house who would never understand a mother's perversity and who would ....

A small sound like a hastily muffled bell, or a quickly stifled cry, broke into and scattered his thoughts, to bring his nerves tight.

He bounced back and forth on the balls of his feet, indecisive at the location of the whispered sound.

He looked toward Mrs. Thurmond. She could hear nothing but the wailing protest of her own soul. He looked toward the maid whose eyes widened in startled bewilderment and turned toward the stairs.

Laine loped across the hall to bound the steps. His hand fumbled in the pocket of his coat and found the butt of the gun. He jerked it against the fold of fabric to bring it into the open, just as he reached the hallway above.

The great space was an anonymous semi-circle with secret doors closed against him. He stood for a moment, poised, every nerve within him listening. A breath of sound pushed him forward to clatter a door wide.

Crouched over the naive bed, fluffy with childhood, bent the interloper, shabby and intent.

Laine pointed the gun in that unaware room, pointed it deliberately and with patient precision. He squeezed the trigger twice and brought thunder into the room. Then he stood waiting, his face cold and hushed, his parted lips rigid against the pointed incisors. Smoke curled from his silent gun.

Barnes' hands rose from his work, the fingers writhing with their unemployment. His body gave a halfhearted twist. His eyes blazed total recognition. Then, with a baffled cry, more of surprise than pain, he slumped to the floor.

Laine gave him a contemptuous stare, walked to the bed and picked up the baby. He unwound the towel and let it drop in a heap of white purity. Lying on the spread, ready for use, lay the phallic symbol—a needle-like knife blade extending beyond the shaft. It was still clean and shiny.

Laine carried the baby to a chair and sat down, cradling her soft limpness in his arms.

Placing an intent ear to the baby lips, he caught a fluttering breath, as delicate as the beating wings of a butterfly, caught and struggling—to tire and give up—then renew the struggle...

Wildly, Laine felt the agitated tremulo of his own body, as he cradled this little one, not knowing how to make the breathing even.

He chafed small hands between his large ones—and looked up and saw in the doorway the maid and the child's pseudo mother. The maid nursed her throat with trembling fingers, her horrified gaze upon the sprawled figure on the floor.

"Goddamn it," shouted Laine in fury, "get out and get that cop in here."

The maid vanished as if given an extemporaneous reprieve from terror. Mrs. Thurmond still stood, looking neither at the child or at the wounded man, but still looking inward at her own bruised life.

"Get downstairs and phone for a doctor." Laine's voice had lowered, his uncontrolled anger winding compactly into a tight-rope of sound.

She looked at him as if she hadn't understood.

"Get that doctor." The rope of sound tautened to quiver with its pull.

Mrs. Thurmond was gone and the doorway yawned emptily.

Barnes' body began to shake, making a small convulsion on the floor. His quiet moans were a monotonous beat against the walls.

Laine rose to pull a blanket from the bed, to halfwrap the baby and lay her on the floor. He bent over her and worked her chubby arms like toy windmills.

He heard a hurried and subdued clatter on the carpet of the stairs. He looked up from his work to the policeman coming in.

"My god! What happened?"

"It was Barnes." Laine jerked his head toward the floor by the bed. "You weren't just seeing things."

The policeman lumbered toward the bed. "Where'd you hit him?"

"In the legs. Got both of 'em. You'll have to get him to a hospital before he loses too much blood."

"How about the baby?"

"Mrs. Thurmond's calling the doctor."

"The hell she is."

Laine looked up, tiny fingers in his hands, chubby arms held upright.

"Sounded to me like she was talking to a lawyer. She said she expected arrest and she had to talk to him. He'd have to bail her out."

"Get down there and jerk her away from the phone. You call a doctor. Get him here in a hurry."

Again Laine was left alone in the room with pain and unconsciousness. Carefully, he worked the child's arms. Gently, he pressed his thumbs methodically upon her chest.

The officer again entered the room. "The maid called the doctor. I went out and got the other boys. Nothin' to watch out there now. One of 'em's with Mrs. Thurmond. The others are on their way up. We'll trundle him down in my car."

"Listen. If you can get in touch with Barclay, have him come out here, will you?"

"Sure will."

CHAPTER THIRTY-TWO

Laine walked slowly down the heavy carpet of the stairs. Barclay waited below. The house was very still with the dead quiet which follows pandemonium.

"How's the little kid?" asked Barclay.

"Better. Much better. The doctor says she's suffering from shock now, and she'll probably have a sore throat for a couple of days…"

"Bet you can't guess who's down at headquarters?"

"I'm not in the mood for guessing," Laine looked coldly at Barclay.

"Thurmond."

"I thought she was still here."

"Not her. Mr. Thurmond. Scottie's stepbrother. The guy that was supposed to get the trust fund."

"Oh?" Laine's voice climbed along with his eyebrows.

"Yeah. We issued a statement to the press this afternoon after the account was decoded and we figured we had the real goods on the racket. It's plastered all over the evening editions."

"Did you tie it up with the murder?"

"No. We're playin' it cagey until the break comes through."

"Uh-huh. Well, now I think it can roll."

"This reporter went out to interview Thurmond for a human-interest angle. Thurmond blew his top and come hot-footin' it down to headquarters for the straight dope. Know what he was worryin' about?"

"All the income she'd spent on the trust fund?"

"Nah. He said it was a rotten trick to play on the kid. He said he wanted to see her, but he wouldn't come out here. Hates the redhead."

"Publicity." Laine's lip curled.

"No, it wasn't. He don't need publicity. He shies from it. They say he gives more to charity on the q.t. than most of these other big shots do with fanfare."

"Okay, then what's he going to do about the baby?"

Barclay grinned, the smile almost changing his expressionless face. "He's gonna make the kid his ward. He says he's gonna see if the courts'll let him adopt her. He'll start proceedings right away. He says her financial status won't change. He'll just switch her from a phony mother to a dad that'll try to be a real one."

"Well," Laine's face softened, lost its tightness. "Well," he repeated, "nice going."

"Mrs. Thurmond and her lawyer are in there…" Barclay jerked his head toward a closed door.

"So what?" Laine regained his weariness. "She's no good. I don't much care what happens to her. Did that gismo get down to headquarters all right?"

"Yeah. They were testin' it when I left. They found dried flakes of something. It'll turn out to be Mary Barnes' blood all right."

"Unless it's chicken blood. You know, that phallic symbol everybody thought was a cross was a clever gimmick. You turned the ring, the knife jumped out…"

Barclay nodded absently.

"How'd that idiot get in here, anyway? The place was guarded. I don't think the maid was in cahoots with him, do you?"

"No. She's in the clear. When I questioned her, she was scared and bewildered. She's okay. Just dumb." Laine thought a moment. "Brand thought he saw a shadow along the wall. He was checking when I drove up. He was a little mad at himself for not being able to figure it out. I think he saw the shadow all right and I've got a hunch on it. Let's go out and look around."

"It's gonna rain any minute."

Laine stepped from the front door. Barclay followed. Both investigators snapped on their flashlights.

Now the wind was roaring through the trees, the sky in angry tumult, black clouds racing beneath the sheet of gray above.

"If the wind don't die down before the rain starts," yelled Barclay, "it's gonna be one hell of a storm."

Laine followed his spot of light down the stone path to the gate. He walked along the inside of the wall. "Can't tell anything," he said loudly, "on this thick grass. But I think Brand saw the shadow through the crevices of the tile. I think Barnes was inside here at the time."

"How'd he get in?"

The wind carried Laine's answer away. He followed the wall, stooping over the circle of light, to the property edge where the tiles turned to continue down the side of the grounds. "Easy to climb," called Laine. "Those holes make good toe-holds."

Suddenly, the light of his flash stopped and Laine played it about on the grass. Small branches and twigs, trampled leaves lay upon the heavy turf. He turned the light on Barclay.

Barclay nodded. "Got through from next door," he agreed loudly. "There's bushes all along there. Maybe it wasn't so hard."

Laine led the way back.

On the terrace, shielded by the house on the one side, the shrubbery on the other, the wind receded to form an island of comparative quiet. "He sneaked along the front wall and followed the shelter of the trellis. Then he waited. When the maid came out and left the front door open, all he had to do was crouch and he'd be out of sight by this terrace wall. He crept into the house and up the stairs." Laine shrugged. "Where've they got him now?"

"In the prison ward of the hospital."

"They were just leg wounds. Let's get busy on him."

Barclay thrust out a hand, palm up. He felt a splatter in its center. "Let's get goin' then. It's startin' to rain. I'll follow you in my heap."

CHAPTER THIRTY-THREE

Laine wrinkled his nose against the hospital smell. An intern lounged with a guard outside the closed door.

"Can we see him?" asked Laine.

The intern pondered. "He's resting comfortably. But he's doped up a little."

"Can he talk?"

The intern grinned. "He can sing. I think the dope made him a little screwy. He keeps singing about blood."

Laine pursed his lips. "No screwier than he was before."

The intern placed his hand on the knob. "Well, if you can make any sense out of him …"

"Enough, I think."

Then the intern remembered his position. "Take it easy, though, will you? You can only have a few minutes. He's a little weak."

"Okay."

Laine and Barclay pushed through.

Barnes looked defenseless in the high bed. His shadowy jaws were lax and thin, twisted lips hung in an inverted semi-circle. The eyes still blazed, but the fanatical light had become indecisive.

"You were trying to kill the child, weren't you?" asked Laine abruptly. "You were trying to strangle Mary's baby for the same reason you killed her mother …"

The loose face gave no flicker of movement or understanding.

"You thought Mary a wicked girl to have loved too much and had a child."

The face remained blank and silent.

Laine walked over to the window to look out upon the dark sky and the bending branches. He stood there stiff and quiet. Then he turned, his expression one of understanding. He walked softly to the bed.

"Every man of us is born in sin and into a wicked world." His voice was hardly above a whisper, the soft words like faded colors delicately woven together to form a subtle tapestry. "In a few of us, there shines a light which guides us on roads of righteousness."

Slowly, the eyes on the bed arced from the ceiling to Laine's scarcely moving lips.

"To those few, with a magnificent power of understanding is given the right to wash away the sin by nothing but the blood."

From between the lax lips on the bed, a tremulous sigh escaped. The lips parted and spoke. "The blood of a harlot and the blood of her bastard shall be the price of their sin together."

The quiet of the room then was as heavy as the odor of medicine. Laine's shoulders drooped as he thought of misguided inspiration and blundering bigotry.

Barclay's thoughts were more direct. His placid face was still expressionless, but rage was beating against his eyes. "For that," he barked suddenly, "you get death from the State."

The face on the pillow smiled. "The executioner himself is immune to penalty."

Laine was beginning to feel a sickness within him rise to gorge his throat. His palms were damp and cold, his brow sweating. He turned and left the room.

Barclay caught up with him in the corridor. "I don't think he will get the gas chamber, either," said Barclay slowly, "I think he'll get the nut house."

"Yes," answered Laine thoughtfully. "It doesn't take an alienist to know he got off the track somewhere along the line."

They reached the outdoors with its winding sheets of rain. They stood on the steps, under the shelter of the overhang, to watch the writhe of the storm.

Barclay stiffened, and placed a hand on Laine's arm. "That wasn't an 'X' on the girl's breast," he said haltingly.

Laine showed no surprise.

"That was a cross." Barclay's face changed from its constant apathy to squeamish horror. With an embarrassed pause in between, it turned again, like remoulding clay to slip back into shielding inertia.

"Yes," said Laine. "A cross—a symbol."

The sweet tones of a Christmas Carol came from the chimes of a downtown church. They trembled through the air over the sound of falling rain.

Barclay hunched the collar of his coat around the face which had given him away. "Well, now," he said patiently, "I'll have a chance to buy those kids' Christmas presents."

"Now they'll be all picked over," said Laine.

Barclay digested this.

"You ought to have a Shopping Service do your leg work for you," suggested Laine. "Like I did. I just picked up the phone and said, 'See here, you get busy and find me a tricycle for a boy about three years old … and a junior tool box that a young fellow can really build things with … and don't forget a doll with real hair for a little princess who likes them pretty!"

Barclay's mouth dropped slowly open.

"They're to be delivered tomorrow. Don't let those little monsters of yours peek, now." Laine slanted his eyes away from Barclay and into the rain again.

"Aw, Laine, you shouldn'ta. Well hell, you're a …"

Barclay cleared his throat. "Jeez, what a storm. Gotta be gettin' home. Can't stand here all night freezin' to death."

He lumbered into the rain.

Laine stood a moment, watching him be swallowed up in the water. Then he, too, left the hospital.